RIDING HIGH WITH KRISHNA
AND A BASEBALL BAT
& OTHER STORIES

RIDING HIGH WITH KRISHNA AND A BASEBALL BAT & OTHER STORIES

Uma Parameswaran

iUniverse, Inc.
New York Lincoln Shanghai

RIDING HIGH WITH KRISHNA AND A BASEBALL BAT & OTHER STORIES

Copyright © 2006 by Uma Parameswaran

iUniverse books may be ordered through booksellers or by contacting:

iUniverse
2021 Pine Lake Road, Suite 100
Lincoln, NE 68512
www.iuniverse.com
1-800-Authors (1-800-288-4677)

ISBN-13: 978-0-595-39438-8 (pbk)
ISBN-13: 978-0-595-83834-9 (ebk)
ISBN-10: 0-595-39438-8 (pbk)
ISBN-10: 0-595-83834-0 (ebk)

Printed in the United States of America

Acknowledgements

"Riding High with Krishna and A Baseball Bat" was first published in Canada by Broken Jaw Press in 2001, with the title *The Sweet Smell of Mother's Milk-Wet Bodice.*

"Savitri" was first published in *Contemporary Verse 2* (Summer 2000). This story is built on and around a story told to me by my cousin, Prema.

"Mooga" is built on and around stories told to me by my sister, Vasanti.

Front Cover Photograph: Purnima Chaudhari

Back Cover Photograph: Peter Tittenberger

Riding High with Krishna and a Baseball Bat

Chapter One

"Okay, girl, come along with me," Krista patted Namita on her back. "Today we'll go for a long drive. Get up, up, and away we go." She gave Namita another hearty push.

As Namita got up from her chair in the living room, Krista looked at her from head to toe. "That cardigan should be enough, it is a warm day. And high time too, seeing July is almost on us. Good you have your runners on, so off we go," she boomed in her cheerful voice. To the receptionist at the front desk, she said she'd step in for a moment to drop off the new girl she was taking with her, but otherwise she was through for the day.

They went to the rear of the building that housed the safe shelter for women, and Krista opened the passenger door of her faded blue Acadian. "Here, hold this till I come around," she pulled out the seat belt and handed the buckle to Namita to hold. She went over to her side, buckled herself in and then reached out to help Namita with the buckle. "Don't worry if you hear this lemon of mine farting like an old horse," she said, "needs a new muffler, may be next month when I get my overtime check. Sometimes you can smell its fart too, some oil leak somewhere, but I can't afford to fix that yet."

They drove along, Krista continuing her cheerful monologue punctuated with hearty laughs. She talked about her grandfather's farm in Gimli, her father's farm in Carman, and chicken and horses and wheat. Namita felt good listening to her. Though she had grown up speaking English at the Christian missionaries' school, Krista's words did not always make sense, with their unfamiliar Canadian accent. Since her arrival, she had not met anyone other than her in-laws, and though the television was on all day, she still had not got used to the accent and pronunciation of the English spoken in this country. But the laugh was wonderful. In these four months, Namita had not heard anyone laugh a real laugh. Menaka, Tarun's brother's wife, laughed often but it was an artificial laugh, a snicker, an ego-filled smirk. The others did not laugh at all, and she had thought she had come to a country where no one laughed, may be laughing was not even allowed. But Krista laughed, laughed often and loudly. It was so wonderful to hear her, so heartwarming.

"Okay, this is Corydon Avenue, and by the time we come back these cafes will be full of people; real lively place they've made this strip in the last few years. Girl, as soon as you get yourself a bus pass, just take a bus, any bus, all day, every day, and see our bejesus beautiful city. Say what anyone may about Winnipeg, we have the best transit system in the country, and I suggest you use it like nobody's business because you don't have to think twice about getting into any bus you want as long as you know which bus to take back home. Or rather, as long as you know you should ask the driver for help as soon as you get in. Yes, girl, you'll soon have a home of your own. Once the long weekend is over, we'll get you started on all the paper work, then you can find out where to get your bus-pass and how to get your résumé ready and soon enough you'll be on your feet, trust me, girl, you *will* be on your feet."

Namita saw that the awnings and cafe tables ended at an intersection at which stood a large church, so like the churches back home, and then the road went on and on, and Krista bubbled on about how Namita will be taken care of, and about women's shelters and welfare forms, and ESL classes, "though you speak English well enough and wouldn't likely need any," she added, and provincial assessment of foreign educational transcripts and how there were jobs a-plenty "So don't you worry, girl. We'll take care of you."

Then she turned right. "This is Assiniboine Park," she said, "you do know, don't you, that we have three rivers—the Red, the Seine—which is a little one—and the Assiniboine. So we have a lot of Assiniboines—Park, Downs, Forest, what have you…" She continued to give a guided tour, starting with the Countess of Dufferin, the engine that stood rather forlornly on its ancient wheels. As they drove by the Conservatory, Namita sat up and Krista said, "This is where you can see your own tropical trees, girl, you can come again when you have the time, and breathe in the humidity of the rain forest, and do look out for the plaque in honor of my late friend, John Serger, who knew just about everything about every plant anywhere in the world, he was my neighbor and a helpful one too, who gave me one of his rare orchid plants, that I have in my office, you can come and see it some time. And this is the Cricket Pavilion, where, if you come by some weekend, you can see them playing, mostly they're from Britain and the Caribbean." Namita's eyes brightened and she could imagine a batsman swinging his bat for a boundary to the cheers of a crowd. Then Krista parked the car and they got out.

The sky was so blue, so vast, Namita drew in her breath. "Are you cold?" Krista asked, "now, if you were like me and had some bum and boobs to speak of, you'd be warmer I bet," and she opened the car door again and drew out a car blanket. "Seems warm enough now but you never know with this bejesus city of ours, even the last week of June can be a dinger. Here, keep this, and I sure hope old Rufus hasn't been pissing on it; just because he can't see any more, he thinks he can get away with peeing where he pleases," she brought it closer to her nose and said, "No, not since I last washed it, anyway."

"I was just looking at the sky," Namita said, "I've never seen so much blue sky in all my life."

"That's another thing about our old city, girl, say what anyone may, we have skies like nobody's business and it is blue three hundred and forty days a year, even when the thermometer drops to thirty below. So, what is the lowest temperature where you're from?"

Namita smiled shyly. "I don't know. In winter, days sometimes get as cold as it is today, and nights are sometimes…I don't know, like in Jaipur we never keep our eyes and ears on the temperature the way the radio does here every few minutes…" her voice trailed away with a catch as she thought of home.

Krista was quick to notice the young woman's choking. "Okay, here we go," she started walking at a rapid clip towards the English Garden. When they came to the Duck Pond, she abruptly sat down on a bench and patted the empty space beside her.

"Girl, you are all out of breath, sit down."

Namita was indeed out of breath, and thankfully sat.

Krista got to her feet right away. "I thought your sneakers would help, but I guess you need more time to learn to walk again; that is what abuse does to you, drops you to your knees and you gotta learn all over again to walk. But we'll take care of that, don't you worry. I haven't jogged all week what with all the graveyard overtime, and I am suffering withdrawal trauma. One's gotta go if one's gotta go." She laughed. "Just a commercial, don't mind me. Now sit right here and I'll go for my jog, okay?"

Namita nodded. "Okay?" Krista said again.

"Okay," Namita said.

"That's better, see you." And she jogged off.

Namita looked at her as long as she could and then clasped her hands. No, there was no need to be afraid. Yesterday she had panicked, for no reason as it turned out.

Krista had taken her for a walk during her coffee break, and she told the receptionist at the desk, "Just going for half an hour, to the river, with Namita here, back soon." But when she realized that Namita had a hard time keeping up, she stopped, looked at Namita's sandaled feet and dramatically flung up her arms. "Jesus, girl, your fancy brocade sandals ain't no walking shoes. You just sit here till I get some fast oxygen into my lungs okay? I am just taking a short fast walk, okay? Won't be long." They were in a small playground.

There were two blond-haired children playing in the sandbox, while the two mothers sat on the swing and chatted with each other. Two older children turned up near the swings, and so the young women got off the swing and perched themselves on either end of the seesaw. Namita marveled at the children's hair; how soft the blond hair was, almost as though they didn't have any, and how it shone like hay in the sun when they turned! The two little ones were so chubby and the two older ones so confident, like the world was theirs for the taking. The world was so beautiful, waiting to be enjoyed. May be, Tarun would appear through the revolving gate that protected this children's enclosure from the rest of the world, and say it was all a mistake, and he would take her home. After all he hadn't been home the last few days, and would have known only now what his parents and brother had done to her. She stared at the gate till her eyes streamed with the strain.

Then Namita panicked. Krista seemed to have vanished. Namita didn't have a clue where this park was with reference to Bournedaya House, and she thought she could not ask anyone because that is the first thing she had been told—no one outside the women's shelter knew where it was because that is the only way women who came there could be really safe. She could not let on that Bournedaya House was within a short walking distance of where she was. But if anyone got really lost, she had been told, they could always phone the crisis line, and she had been given a sheet with the phone number. But she had crushed the paper and thrown it away.

Menaka had given her a similar piece of paper with phone numbers, was it only twenty four hours ago? Menaka was married to Tarun's older brother, Bhaiyan. In the afternoon, after the parents-in-law had retired for their after-lunch nap as though nothing had happened to affect their routine, Menaka had come from her bedroom upstairs and sat next to Namita, in the dreary living room with its oversized red sofas and drapes with ugly huge flowers. Menaka had whispered that there were places Namita could go to, and she had offered her a sheet on which were written words and phone numbers—Women's Advocacy, Immigrant Women's Association of Manitoba, Immigrant Women's Employment Counseling, International Center, Salvation Army. "Phone one of these," she whispered, "they can help."

"Help get him back?" Namita asked.

Menaka smirked. "No, not him, but they can help you survive when you get thrown out. Phone them now, while you have a phone. Here, keep these too," and she rummaged through her handbag and thrust eight quarters into Namita's palm forcing her hand open. "So you can phone me at this time any day, when they are sleeping," she gestured towards the old couple's room. And then she walked up the stairs to her room. She had a mincing walk, her left hip swayed more than her right, and her silver anklets seductively tinkled. Namita felt gooseflesh of fear all over her arms. What did she mean, when she got thrown out?

That morning, at 10:58, as noted on the paper that still lay on the night table next to her bed, she had been served divorce papers. The courier had come to the door, and her father-in-law had greeted him cordially as one would a long-expected visitor. He took the envelope, sheet and pen that the man handed him, and extending the sheet and pen to Namita said, "Just sign your name here." Thinking it was a parcel from India, she eagerly took the sheet and signed it. Even as she handed it over to the man, she read the words, "Received a copy of the Petition," and suddenly realized this man was not a mailman, and that these papers held danger. She snatched it back from the man, and ran towards the kitchen. She would not accept the envelope, no matter what it contained, that her father-in-law held in his hand. She stood at the kitchen door, sheet in hand. As long as she did not sign for it, he could not give it to her, whatever it was. "Give it at once," her father-in-law barked at her. She crumpled the sheet and closed her fist around it. She would not accept whatever it was that they were forcing on her. If they wanted her to have it, it was something bad. But the man left it anyway. Carefully poising a new delivery sheet on his knee, he wrote something, handed it to her father-in-law, and left.

She stumbled to her room and sat on her bed while Menaka and her mother-in-law set about preparing lunch. Her father-in-law came into her room, placed the envelope on the bed next to her, and went out, closing the door behind him.

Namita took out the sheaf of papers from the envelope that her father-in-law had already opened. The top sheet was a copy of what she had crumpled. The courier had written, "REFUSED TO SIGN," and "10:58 a.m." The cover sheet of the stapled sheaf of papers read "PETITION FOR DIVORCE."

Everyone went on as though nothing had happened. While she sat on the bed in her room, they had lunch, washed up, and the parents-in-law went for their afternoon nap. She had come out of her room and sat in the living room with its ugly drapes. Menaka had joined her and given her a sheet of paper with the name and phone number of the various agencies.

That is why Namita had crumpled up the page with the phone number of Bournedaya House crisis line that the counselor had given her.

And now, as she sat in the children's playground, she did not know where she was or where she could go or what she should do as she sat on the bench where Krista had left her. One of the children was curious about her and circled his way towards her, but his mother called him back. No one wanted her, not her husband's family, not these strangers, and only Krista kept saying everything would be taken care of, and Krista had disappeared. Namita sat petrified on the bench, staring and staring at the poplar that was shutting out the sun. A scream was working its way up her throat from the pit of her stomach. But it did not emerge; instead, she could feel its python coils stretching from inside her larynx and choking her. She wanted to scream and scream and get it all out, but no sound came. And then Krista had appeared, her T-shirt all wet with sweat and a big grin on her face. She sat next to Namita, and said, "Jeesus, I feel better now, not as good as if I'd really jogged but a fast walk is okay too. I'll get you some walking shoes when we get back."

Krista had got her the cardigan and runners yesterday night, and now here she was, in someone else's shoes. Surely surely they were not hers for long; Tarun would find her and ask her to throw back these unsightly clothes that Krista had fished for her from a closet in the Counselors' Room and he would take her back home.

Namita pulled the cardigan closer around herself on feeling a sudden breeze. The cardigan was way too big for her, and she had rolled the sleeves four inches up; the base color was a dull gray, but there were Fair-Isle patterns and bright geometric diamonds of blue, and a red line running through the diamond. Krista called these pants *sweat pants*, and they were just like Krista's, fleecy navy pull-ons.

On the duck pond, there were no birds. Some children, on parent's leash peered in, looking for fish, and then they went away, parent and children pretending to chase each other. Soon after, four birds flew in and circled overhead, flapping their brown wings as they came down in a slow spiral. They landed on the surface of the pond, and suddenly they were not brown any more. Bright turquoise lined their back between the brown, and on either side of the neck flashed a brilliant patch of peacock blue. And now their heads were green, now dark blue. They floated without disturbing the surface, as though they were part of a still life painting. And then some children ran towards the water, parents in tow, wanting to feed popcorn to the birds, which now paddled away to the farther end of the pond.

Peacock blue. Namita's memory raced home to Jaipur.

Not far from the gates of her father's house was a place they called the peacock garden. It was on an estate owned by Seth Govind Das, with a house recessed on the far side. A wicket gate allowed public access to the private garden. At the center was a shallow pond, fed by rain water, but it was often dry. Radiating from it were paths of fine golden sand that shimmered like waves when the sun was blazing, but in the mornings and late afternoons the sand was fine and cool under their bare feet. Along the path that led to the house were tall *ashoka* trees, their slender trunks and conical shapes reaching upwards. The other paths had flowering trees, bougainvillea of deep pink, great big *gulmohurs* with their flaming orange-red flowers. Closer to the house were creepers of jasmine and *raat-ki-rani* and *chameli*, their delicate fragrance welcoming visitors to the private compound of the house. The estate was surrounded by a hedge of thorny *keekar* and cactus-like bushes which kept the cattle from entering the garden. They stretched their twisted branches in different directions like the hood of a snake.

At one end of the garden was a mesh enclosure. Inside were four peacocks and as many peahens. This was a favorite haunt for the children in the neighborhood. They spent hours watching the birds. These peacocks seemed to open their fans every time their master came near the enclosure. At other times they would strut their fan on whim, and not just when rain clouds gathered as songs and stories always said.

Namita and her sister Asha, and later her brothers as well, would stand entranced, watching the birds lazily drawing their long brown tails behind them, the feathers all bunched together so that the bright eyes on their tails did not stand out. Then one would stop, turn around once or twice, and twitch his tail and slowly lift it, spreading his fan in a glorious circle of swirling blue and green and purple. He would solemnly move towards a peahen, and stand still. Or he would come close to the children and slant his head sideways. Sometimes, the peacocks would suddenly close their fan and run, their raucous shrill cry scaring the wits out of the children. It happened every time, the chill of fear when that raucous cry split their ears.

Seth Govind Das, the rich old man who owned the garden, had another obsession as well. He had statues of Lord Krishna all over the garden. Of different kinds and sizes. Of stone and clay and wood and terra cotta and ceramic. In different poses, but the majority standing in the familiar pose of crossed feet, flute at mouth. Some were broken at the edges, some worn flat as though dredged from the bottom of the sea. Many were crude, made by stonecutters rather than sculptors, but the old man bought any statue anyone brought to his door. He fed these artists, even if they only pretended to be one so they could get access to his legendary hospitality. They would stay a few weeks, chipping away at one or other rock on the estate. They were given two meals a day, and a blanket.

At the far end of the garden was his house, separated from the public section by a three-foot high hedge of green. Along the verandahs and in the small front courtyard were the more artistic statues, and only special neighbors were invited to come here. Namita's family was special. Their mother often sent, through the girls, food and festival sweets for the old man, for he had no family of his own locally who could provide the kind of home-cooked food their mother could. Their mother also sent him a bowl of whatever special offering she made to God everyday in her *pooja* room. He, in turn, would give them dry-fruits and flowers to take back to their mother. He loved children, especially Namita and her siblings, whom he saw everyday, unlike his grandchildren who came on short visits, never long enough for them to be at ease with him.

He lived alone, with a houseful of retainers who cooked and cleaned and spent all their days tending the garden. His grown sons and daughters lived in Delhi, where they had a family business that he had started long ago and handed over to them. During the winter months, they periodically drove down with their entourage, stayed a day or two at a time, and went back.

One day, when Namita and Asha excitedly told him about the upcoming wedding of the older sister of one of their friends, he told them that when they got married, he would give each of them a statue of their choice. Close to the front door of his house was a Krishna of black granite, exquisitely chiseled, almost life size. Namita pointed to the black Krishna that was clearly the old man's most treasured piece, and laughingly said, "Even that one? Will you give me even that one if I choose?" and he said, "Certainly, as long as you promise you will carry it away carefully to your husband's house."

It was a conversation they repeated and shared. But one day, Namita decided to be smart. Even at that age, she was more practical than Asha, and had figured out a bird in hand was worth two in the bush. "Why don't I just take a baby Krishna now instead of the big one later?" and he had said, "Fair enough," and she had chosen a wooden Krishna about a foot high. For months she had carried it around, dressed it and fed it, pretending she was Princess Meera, who had carried around just such a statue and become Lord Krishna's favorite friend so that he came whenever she called him. Then she had stood it on a table in her room.

Now, she thought longingly of that statue. Bina-ma would be taking good care of it, she knew. Bina-ma. Namita sighed. How far away she was from Bina-ma, mother who was not her mother and yet more than mother.

Namita was six and Asha eight when their mother started dying. She took a long time to die. There were months of intense pain, followed by months of remission but the fear was always there even when she was in remission. The girls were old enough to feel the stress, and they walked softly and spoke in whispers even when Mother was well enough to do all the usual chores of braiding their hair, serving Pappaji's meals, and overseeing the housework that was done by two different maids who came at different times so that at least one was around at any given time. She died two months after Asha had got her first period; it was as though she had been keeping herself alive to see her daughter through that step. "You have to tell all that I tell you now to Namita when the time comes," she had said.

But Asha did not have to. Their father got married again six months later.

Suddenly home was bright and cheerful again. Bina was only eight years older than Asha, and so they worked out a compromise to add Ma to her name instead of calling her by her name, which was not done, or calling her Ma (they were not ready to do that) or Chhoti Ma (Little Mother). Bina was a strong young woman, with strong hands, big teeth, high jawbones and a laugh that made the girls' world bright. They went off to the bazaar every weekend, and bought all kinds of ribbons and hair clips and beads and bangles over which they played and quarreled together. Though Bina-ma did not join in their skipping rope games, for she got pregnant within months of arriving, she would play every other game with them and their friends. Soon after Pappaji brought Bina home, whenever the girls visited neighbors or relatives, they would hear commiseration and pity poured on them for being motherless and orphaned, and they would listen to more covert hints by the well-meaning nosy-pokes of how sad it was that Father had re-married before the poor woman's ashes had got cold. Then they would come home and mimic to Bina-ma what they had been told, and all three would laugh and laugh till their stomachs hurt.

But Bina-ma was Mother too. She kept the house clean and tidy at all times, and trained the girls in kitchen work. She arranged for a music Master to come home to give singing-lessons, and made them teach her the songs after the Master left, even though she had a tone-deaf ear that could not pick up any nuances. She packed off the cook and taught the girls to help her in the kitchen every day. She was always laughing but she had all of them, including Pappaji, under her thumb. In quick succession, two brothers, Akhil and Nikhil, appeared. Over the next few years, the girls doted on the little boys, and they in return worshiped their sisters. Even as toddlers, they knew when to expect the girls home from school, and they'd be all ready and impatient to be taken out for a walk to Sethji's peacock garden. Sethji loved all of them, and whenever he was not busy with something else, he would carry the baby, hold the other by hand, and all of them would walk to the peacocks and watch the proud display.

Namita could see the peacocks in these small birds in front of her, the cerulean blue darting from their necks as they floated by with little movements of neck and webbed feet.

If she were to ask Krista to let her phone Jaipur, Bina-ma would arrange for her flight home; she was sure of that, though she knew her father had already dipped into his retirement fund in order to buy her the ticket the first time. There had been talk about how it was almost as cheap to buy a return flight as a one-way flight, but Bina-ma had been against it; a bride who was on her way to live with her husband should not have a return ticket. Bina didn't want to say aloud that it was a bad omen; instead she said that girls should know that their new home was where they belonged.

Yes, Bina-ma would sell her own bangles if need be to arrange for a ticket. But no, Namita would not ask. Surely Tarun would come around, surely all this was a mistake, and the only way she could make sure it was a mistake was to stay right here and wait for Tarun.

Tarun would never have allowed what had happened to happen. Around three o'clock, after their nap, which the others had taken as though nothing out of the ordinary had happened, Menaka and her father in law had come into her room, and asked her to pack. They had brought in her second suitcase, which had been stowed in the basement, and they had opened the closet doors and told her to pack her things. At which, she had started crying. They had shut the door and gone to have their afternoon tea, and snacks.

In the closet was her locked Samsonite suitcase, given as part of her trousseau, in which most of the elaborately embroidered salwar suits and saris still lay untouched. There had been no occasion to wear any of them. Her mother in law went out with her husband for a walk every day after the afternoon tea, and Menaka and Bhaiyan often went out late evenings, but Namita was kept secluded. From her Samsonite, she had taken out a couple of her silk saris, her favorite parrot green Banarsi silk, and yellow and red Conjeevaram, and worn them in the evenings just before Tarun's usual time for returning from work. These and other artificial silks hung in the closet. Her everyday salwar suits lay folded on closet shelves. Namita closed the closet door, sat on her bed and cried.

She cried all the way to dinner-time; her mother in law came in and said, "Please don't cry, please don't cry, you are making me feel so sorry, please." And then her father in law had dragged his wife away forcibly, had come back and bellowed, "Don't you see how you are making poor Ma-ji ill? Get going, quick."

She continued to cry, and Menaka came in and threw all her saris and suits into the suitcase. When she came to the parrot-green sari that Namita had worn for the wedding reception, Menaka held it against herself and said, "This is Tarun's favorite color, may be I'll keep it safe for you." Namita hurled herself against the other woman in a sudden fit of recognition.

At the Reception, as they sat on the bedecked throne-like chairs side by side, Tarun had told her about that color being his favorite, how coincidental it was that she had chosen his favorite color, and she had thought it a good omen, that they would be in synch forever and forever.

"Don't you dare, don't you dare touch my sari," Namita clawed at Menaka in unbridled grief, snatching back the sari. Menaka turned away with a shrug. "Who cares? You can keep all your saris, not that I can see any use for them where you are going to be. You keep your saris, and I'll keep your..." she drawled, leaving her sentence unfinished.

Menaka was like that, full of innuendoes. Over the last four months, she had needled Namita with subtle and not-so-subtle hints about Tarun's eyes and hands that couldn't keep away from nice-looking women. And why not, she had said quite openly; who would want a featherless crow when one could have a cute *koel*? Menaka was proud of her looks, her little turned up nose and chubby face with deep dimples on both cheeks, and she thought Namita plain. Often she would dismiss Namita's choice of colors, drawling that the color itself was lovely but surely Namita knew it was not right for her.... These exchanges always took place in the living room, after the in-laws had retired for their nap. Namita could never figure out just what Menaka had implied until afterwards, when she thought about the exchanges. The words were always double-edged; they implied that it was well known around town that Tarun was a womanizer; but they could also be read as that she and Tarun had a relationship that was special, that she came first at all times and would for all time, and that she was the only woman in his life.

Namita had brooded over these exchanges, had tried to give excuses for her husband at every turn—he liked to enjoy life, have a drink and a cigarette when he came home, he was just being more free with Menaka because he knew her more, she having been here a whole lot longer than Namita. Most of all, he was being pressured by his family to keep away from his wife, and so could not show her any affection as long as his parents were around. That was it. His family. Once he got out of their clutches, he would be all right; meanwhile, if he chose to flirt with his sister-in-law, well, it would pass. He would come around. It was only a matter of time. She would be patient. With these and similar rationalizing, she had explained away so many things that seemed beyond her.

Their living arrangements had upset her, but she knew the reason why her in-laws were so against her, and was willing to wait. While Bhaiyan and Menaka had the master bedroom upstairs that occupied the entire floor of the one and a half level house, and the parents had their bedroom on the ground floor, she and Tarun had only a small room with a single bed. Tarun kept his clothes and books in a closet at the back. He always went out after dinner and came back very late. Quickly, furtively, he would slide into her bed, make love and leave for his couch in the living room. Very often he was away for a couple of days; it was his work, he said, he had to be on the road a lot.

She had realized that his salary of $1500 a month was far from a princely sum in Canada. She suspected that he was doing some very menial job that he did not want to talk about. But she had accepted that. One had to start on the lowest rung of the ladder and work one's way up. As she was willing to, in her climb into her in-laws' hearts.

There were many things she could not understand about her new family. But she had thought she would get accepted one day, once they got over the wrangle about her dowry. And then had come the divorce papers. Go back, they had said, go back the way you came here. Since you didn't wait for your husband to send you a ticket, you can go back on your own too.

She would stay on in Winnipeg. Girls should know that their new home was where they belonged.

Krista was back. They sat side by side on the bench for a few minutes. Then Krista rose with her usual "Let's get the work done" efficiency and led the way to the car.

"Let us take another route going back," she said. "You've got to see where the *beautiful people* live." She slowly drove along the road between vast stretches of grass where a great many people in colorful shorts and T-shirts were walking with children or by themselves. These were beautiful people, indeed, Namita had never seen so much of bare skin among people of her own class. Peasants and working class men wore hardly anything back home, but the women here were just so bare and beautiful, it took her breath away. But then, everything was taking her breath away. It was all so new, all so wonderful, and Krista was the most wonderful of all, large-hearted Krista sitting by her and bubbling away about Wellington Crescent houses as they left the Park. As they drove past the manorial houses, Namita realized what Krista meant by *beautiful people.*

"Look to your left," Krista said, breaking into Namita's thoughts, "ain't that a beauty or what? One day, girl, you and me'll buy it, what says you?" Namita looked at the house—it was something vaguely familiar, that she had grown up with, but she couldn't place it immediately—the brownstone, the castle like square tops and gables, the narrow vertical windows on the walls speckled with stone-like projections, the high wrought-iron gates.

"Shakespeare," she said, pleased that it had come to her. "Shakespeare's England," she saw the old school texts that her father had used in his school days, and that she had read when she was in school with such delight to her little brothers even though their vocabulary was all of twenty words.

"What you talking about, girl? Where did you read about Shakespeare and all?"

"In school and college, doesn't every one?"

Krista whistled. This young woman knew Shakespeare. She should be okay soon, then. On first seeing her, Krista had thought she was totally helpless, with her outlandish clothes and heavy gold jewelry, and silver-work sandals, but if she knew Shakespeare, and since she spoke English well enough, she'd be okay. Krista wondered about this young woman, rather different from others, who had come to their door step. She had been at the desk when the call came through, first from the Salvation Army Crisis Line and then from the girl herself. A garbled story, full of sobs and pauses, saying she had nowhere to go, her family had thrown her out (at which there were voices in the background shushing her up), she was a new immigrant, and had got their phone number from the Salvation Army Crisis Line. Krista had asked for her address so she could send a taxi, and again there were voices in the background and then Namita's that she'd be at the 7-Eleven at the corner of Leila and McPhillips.

Which is where Namita's brother-in-law had deposited her. He had sat in his car until the taxi came and then he had taken off.

Krista had tried to trace the call, but it had been blocked, and she knew at that moment that she was dealing with double-dyed crooks who knew all the rules and how to break them with impunity.

Now, as they drove over Maryland Bridge, she said, "Girl, those men in your family, they are devils incarnate, they blocked their number before they made you call, didn't they?"

Namita said she did not know what that meant. "Never mind," Krista said, "never you mind, you'll be okay."

Namita thought of how she had been forced to make that call to Bournedaya House. Her father-in-law and brother-in-law had stood over her and asked her to phone the Salvation Army crisis line, and she had resisted them for an hour, crying in a wild paroxysm that kept them away, but the moment her paroxysm had spent itself, they had twisted her arm literally, and had dialed the number, had listened in while she was given the Bournedaya House crisis line; they had then asked her to dial the number, and she had refused. They had left her alone for a while. Even in all the trauma of the situation, she had figured out that if she did not speak, they would be at a loss; not that it had prevented the man from delivering the *Petition for Divorce*, she thought. But clearly her resistance did mean something, and so she resisted. Meanwhile it was getting dark. Even the long June day had to end.

The two men stood over her as she cowered on the ugly red sofa. They told her she did not know the law of this land; if they phoned the police and complained that she was an intruder, an illegal alien, the police would take her away, lock her up, send her back to where she came from. To Gehunnum, they added, because that was where she belonged, in hell. They had her passport, all the papers concerning her education, degrees, and she could dance herself lame (even in that moment they thought to stab at her with her Master's in Music and Dance degree that was her pride). But if she behaved herself, she could take everything she had brought with her, passport, saris and all. They did not mention her jewelry, which they had appropriated soon after the wedding.

Even in her wild grief and helplessness, she had figured out (wrongly, as Krista told her later) they had a trump card—the threat of deportation; if the police got her, she would never see Tarun again. She had to be in Winnipeg, when Tarun came back from wherever he was. He would come back.

So she had asked for her passport. "Don't you trust us, you bitch?" her brother-in-law had said. No, she wanted to say, never. But she had only repeated, Give me my passport, and they had given it to her. Then she had dialed the number they had wanted her to.

❦   ❦   ❦

When they entered the foyer, the receptionist got up and ran to Krista, "Thank God you are here, Krista, do we ever need you. Alina is back, and pregnant too."

Krista rushed to the anteroom, forgetting all about Namita, who followed her.

Alina was half reclining on the four-seat sofa. Her arm was bandaged in blood-soaked segments of a bed sheet, her left eye had disappeared in a monstrous swelling and she lay with one eye open, looking at her children. They seemed to be about ages four and six. They stood on either side of her knees, staring at her solemnly with their big black eyes. Their brown hair was tightly curled on their head. They were beautiful little children, their solemn eyes holding the unarticulated pain of ages.

Krista dropped to her knees and gathered them up. "My, my, my," she said, "I am so glad to have you back. I've missed you guys like nobody's business. Your Royal Highness Robby, and Your Royal Highness Deena? Come, come, do you remember your own little room from before? The one with little birdies on the drapes, right?"

The solemn eyes turned to her and then they smiled, the smile working slowly down to their mouths. They closed their eyes, and murmured against her breast, as children do when they are safely cuddled.

"He was laid off," Alina said. "It's not his fault. A man who cannot feed his family gets broken."

"And so he breaks his wife's bones?" Krista said softly.

"He is a good man," Alina said stubbornly.

Krista released the children, and said softly, "Now my most favorite little Robby and Deena are going to have something to eat before they go to bed, right? Joan will help you choose what you want to eat, now go with her and I'll take care of Mama."

They turned their eyes to their mother again, and leaned over her knee. They would not leave her. Krista cradled them again, crooning them to safety.

Namita went to her room, sat on her bed, and cried as she had never cried before. She then curled herself into as small a space as she could, and cried into her pillow.

Krista came in at some point, and Namita woke up. Krista sat on the empty bed next to Namita's, and said, "Come, girl, if you want to go to bed without supper, go ahead, but the least you could do is get under the covers, right?" Namita pulled herself up and flung her arms around Krista. How soft her bosom was, and how gentle her hands. Namita remembered the times she nestled into Bina-ma's bosom, always wet with milk, with the sour-sweetness of milk that had dried on the bodice. Bina-Ma nursed her children well into their second year, and even longer for the older one, who was jealous if he could not get to her the same time his brother did.

Krista allowed her to take comfort. "Makes me feel almost guilty when I go home to my family," she said. "And you can take heart, I guess, that you have not been beaten black and blue."

Krista waited. This young woman will bounce back sooner than most, she thought. It was something about her, her sense of wonder at this new world. It would be so good, she thought, if this young woman would come back and help out once she was on her feet. But she would not hold her breath on that. These Asian women, they were a secretive bunch; never wanted to let on they had ever been in a shelter, or on welfare. Something about their culture, she supposed, that made them disappear the moment they had been helped to their feet. Never wanted to recognize each other, either, like Farzana who had vanished from the lounge the moment she saw that the newcomer two nights ago was also brown skinned. If these women would just realize didn't have to feel ashamed simply because their partners were devil's own double-dyed jerks, if they would just recognize each other and share their stories, if they could just spread the word that there was help available and no woman need put up with shit…. No, the few Asian women who did find their way here vanished as soon as they could and never came back, or even sent an anonymous thank you card. Never mind, as long as they got back on their feet, Krista thought, always generous in her reactions.

Chapter Two

The next morning, Namita was told she had been assigned a Counselor from Immigrant Women's Association of Manitoba, who would soon visit her. She sat in the lounge all morning, waiting for her. Shayna was quite unlike Krista in many ways, but she was caring and supportive in her own quiet way. A small-made woman in her forties, she spoke slowly and softly in a measured voice and tone. She took down a great many routine details of Namita's background: when and where she was married, when she had got her sponsorship papers, when she had arrived. She carefully went through the divorce papers, and said, "Have you gone through these papers? Don't worry, you don't need to. I think the first thing we have to do is to get you a Legal Aid lawyer. Once the long weekend is over, we can get started. I shall arrange that you continue to stay here for a few days."

In the lunchroom was a large notice, asking everyone to be there at three o'clock to listen to Krista, whose shift started late afternoon. While the others went away after lunch, Namita stayed on, counting the minutes to three o'clock when she could see Krista' friendly face again and talk about her morning meeting with Shayna.

Krista came in exactly at three o'clock, a tornado of energy. She greeted everyone by name, held Robby and Deena by hand, and announced that everyone, who wished to, would go to the Forks at eight o'clock and stay till the fireworks. Seeing Namita's surprised look, she turned to Robby and said, "My little man, do you think you could explain to this young lady what we are celebrating?" Solemnly, he whispered, "Canada Day."

"And what is that?" "Canada's birthday," piped in a happier child. "Birthday candles, birthday cake" "Right-oh, and songs and fireworks, eeoo." The children in the room got excited. Their mothers smiled wanly. Counselors got everyone to join hands, and they danced in and out, side to side, any way they chose, pulling and pushing the circle in different directions.

That evening, there were a whole lot of new people, men and women, waiting to take them out to the Forks. "Where's everyone?" Krista boomed. There weren't too many inmates assembled. Those with children were there, and Robby and Deena in Jeanne's care without their mother, but Krista felt there should be more. On the intercom, she boomed, "Okay people, you have a choice: you can mope in the corner of your room, you can watch the show on TV or you can come with us and join some real fun."

Several more women came out in the next few minutes. Krista gave a little talk about exactly what they would do, who was in charge of whom, who was to hold whose hands and never let go, and introduced the volunteers. "Say what anyone may," she boomed, "our Winterpeg is the world's greatest volunteerism capital, as you can see. Let's give them a hand." The women clapped half-heartedly.

When the evening was over, and the children asleep on parent or volunteer shoulders, one of the mothers thanked the volunteers, and there were hugs and handshakes all around, and the clapping went on and on, waking some of the children, who were crooned back to sleep. Rick, one of the volunteers, sat on the sofa holding sleeping Robby and Deena on his lap, waiting for someone to take them to their room.

The receptionist came to Namita and said Tarun had called earlier, had said he would call again, and she should wait for his call and not do anything till then. A great load lifted from her heart. Tarun was back. All was well. He would clear up this terrible nightmare. She quickly deciphered his message as that he knew everything that had happened to her, but was still under his family's control and so she should not call him at his brother's home. She was relieved. She understood it perfectly. She would be patient.

Her first Canada Day in this country had turned out to be a real birthday party, after all. The world was a safe place, just as it had been in the days of Bhagavan Rama.

Namita remembered as her most treasured memories those winter evenings when the boys were toddlers. During the day, cooking was done on the gas and electric stoves on the cooking table. In the evenings, Bina-Ma had two coal *sigris* lit by the maid before she left. About the time Pappaji returned from work, she would put the *dal*-pot on one stove and the vegetable skillet on the other, and both would cook on the very slow heat for as long as the children needed to play with their dad, or do their homework. When it was time for dinner, she would sit on the wooden *paat* next to the sigris, take down the vegetable skillet and replace it with the chapatti skillet, and start rolling out the dough that the maid had kneaded and covered. The girls would set out the plates, tumblers of water, paats to sit on, and clap a spoon on a plate to call the "men-folk" and Pappaji would come in, the boys hanging at his knees, and all would sit in a circle around the warm sigri.

Bina-Ma would serve them hot chapattis, thin and soft, topped with ghee, and they would eat and chat, chat and eat. After everything was put away, they would continue to sit around the warm sigris, now with no pot on them but the coal almost spent. The girls would sit on either side of Bina-Ma leaning into her, and the boys would be on their father's lap. Then Bina-Ma would open her Ramayana and tell them a story each day. Her volume had a great many colored pictures, and the girls would open the page to where the tassel bookmark was, so they could start each evening where they had left off the previous evening.

Bina-Ma never read from the book; rather she would retell the story with her own digressions, and always find places to insert something about Pappaji; every good quality any hero or heroine had in the story came right around to Pappaji; the girls were old enough to recognize in a distant way that Bina-Ma's interpolations were naughty, and referred to something that happened between their parents in private moments. It gave them great joy to know they were part of whatever it was that was happening between their parents around the warm sigri, while the boys slept in their father's lap, and the colors jumped off the page on their mother's lap and Bhagavan Ramachandra and his happy monkey-friends marched onward to Lanka so the world could be a safe place for everyone.

Two days went by, and Tarun still had not called. Everything was closed for the long weekend that went on to Monday. Namita stayed in all the time, to be sure she was there when the telephone call came. Newspaper on her lap, she was calm. Her in-laws being what they were, she could imagine what had happened. Tarun would have been out-talked, and they would have raked up the whole wrangle over her dowry.

Pappaji was an austere man in some ways. He belonged to a group led by a progressive swami who advocated a simple life of honesty and hard work. No smoking, no drinking, no meat-eating, no dishonest deals in business or in personal life. Big deal, Bina-Ma would say dismissively of all the forbidden pleasures, who has the time for all that anyway?

When Asha turned eighteen, marriage talks became the daily dinner conversation. Pappaji always started off with his dictum of refusing any prospective alliances which did not meet his "No smoking, no drinking, no meat eating" criteria, and Bina-Ma would intervene along the lines of "He has to be almost as handsome as Pappaji, because no one can be more good-looking...." and look with dancing eyes at her husband. Bina-Ma had a way of flirting with him in the presence of the girls because they had been there from her day one, and she had figured she'd make it part of the family's togetherness.

Within six months, they had a match, a perfect match, so the astrologers maintained. The young man was an engineer, the eldest son of Seth Ram Prasad, who came from an old Jaipur family. They lived at the other end of the city, but it was a comfort that their Asha would be in the city of her birth after all.

The families met several times. Once, they visited at Bina-Ma's invitation. Pappaji was dead against such an occasion saying he would have none of anything that bore even a whiff of commercial negotiations, but Bina-Ma had her way. It is best to talk about their expectations face to face, she said. She wanted to show them the jewelry Asha would be getting, and that would open up conversation about what else they expected. She did not use the tabooed word, "dowry."

So there they were one Wednesday afternoon, Seth Ram Prasad and his wife, and a sister of hers. After hot pakoras stuffed with choice cashews, and steaming hot jalebis, and masala tea, the men sat on chairs and talked whatever men talk about, and the women sat on a silk mat, where Bina-Ma had spread out the jewelry. The jewelry sets lay in two large trays, in open velvet-lined boxes. There were three complete sets of necklace, earrings and bangles on each tray, and several other single pieces of gold chains and pendants and bracelets. She explained that this was the jewelry left by the girls' mother (may her soul be at peace), all the jewelry she had owned, she said that several times so it would sink in that she was not keeping any for herself. She had made it into two equal halves, one for each of the girls. Asha's parents-in-law could choose which half they wanted, though she herself favored the one with the jade set because jade was Asha's lucky stone.

At this point, Seth Ram Prasad dragged his chair towards the women, and leaned forward. He carefully picked up the jade set and placed it on the coffee table next to his chair. "Exquisite, exquisite," he said, "and all the more dear for having been worn by a good woman, may her soul be at peace. Lalaji, it is a good omen indeed because jade is my family's lucky stone as well, and I insist on giving our daughter-in-law a jade set on her wedding day. For, let me be frank with my fears, Lalaji, jade is a 'nakhra' gem, a whimsical stone, and its flaws latch on to the wearer. We have a family jeweler who is the best connoisseur of jades Jaipur has ever known, and we shall pick perfect flawless gems, be sure of that. Not that I mean to say anything less than the best about this blessed lady's perfect set, Lalaji, but I have taken a vow that we shall give a jade set to each daughter in law who enters our home. And so," he put the jade set on the farther tray and transferred a ruby set from it to the tray to his left.

"Very generous of you, Seth, very generous, my daughter is lucky indeed."

"Not at all, Lalaji, all of us want our children's happiness do we not? And now," (he said the Now with a deliberate pause as though to say "Listen") he took a pearl set from the right tray and exchanged it with an amethyst set on the left. "Pearls and rubies go well together. This way, she can mix and match the two sets."

"Of course, of course, good taste, Sethji."

Soon both trays were on the coffee table. One by one, he picked up the jewelry and if he made an exchange, he gave a very beautifully worded explanation to which Pappaji gladly nodded acquiescence. He surveyed the new arrangement and stretched it towards the ladies so they could admire his choice.

"And now," he turned to Pappaji. "Lalaji, you are a *sharif* person, all of Jaipur knows, and so I can say this to you without being misunderstood. Your late blessed wife, may whose soul be at peace, has given much. And it is right that you share it between your daughters equally. But have you considered this? That may be you could give each of them a complete set of her jewelry, half hers and the other half replicas of the rest? Think how happy it would make each of your lovely daughters, to have a complete set of their dear mother's jewelry. Now, my family jeweler has the best workers in all of Jaipur, and he can make a duplicate set perfect in every detail." From the jhola (cloth bag) he had brought, he extracted mesh bags, one red and the other green. The girls watched from the doorway, fascinated that he should have exactly what he wanted in his bag. He carefully slid each tray into one of the bags, which being fine mesh, enlarged just enough to cover it snugly. "So here it is, behn-ji," he gestured to Bina-ma to take them away. "The red bag is our daughter's blessed mother's jewelry, and in the green one are the pieces which our jeweler will duplicate for you so you can add them to our daughter's. I'll phone our jeweler tomorrow and we can fix up a time to visit his shop. I will myself drive you there, Lalaji, and of course behn-ji too if she so wishes."

"Of course, of course," Pappaji said. "Very kind of you, sir, very kind indeed."

"Now, one more detail, if I may, Lalaji, for you are a sharif man and will listen patiently. Over the last decades, I have gone to numberless marriages in my extended family, Lalaji, and this is to be the first in my own house. I would very much want everyone, no matter how far they are, to attend this happy occasion. So sending them tickets would help, don't you think? Not airfare or anything like that. Just first class train fare would do."

"Of course, of course," Pappaji said.

"Now, let us see. Thirty thousand cash should do, I think. I will take care of any extra that might be needed. Thirty thousand?"

"Certainly, no problem," Pappaji said.

❧   ❧   ❧

When Pappaji returned from the gate after seeing them off, Bina-Ma was in a classic pose of mockery—finger on cheek, rolling eyes—and the girls were holding their sides laughing.

"Chup, stop. What have I got myself into? If that wasn't a dowry-session, what was it? It is all your fault."

Bina-Ma laughed it away. "Don't fret so much, Lalaji, I know you are a sharif person." And all three young women laughed and laughed till their stomachs hurt. But Bina-Ma pulled short, and said in a serious voice, "Don't fret. I told you it is best to be up front about it. After all dowry is just the way of making sure daughters also, and not just the sons, get a share of their father's property."

"Old ways have to change, dowry is illegal, and I'll be damned if I marry my daughter to anyone barbaric enough to demand dowry."

"Ssh. They are nice people, believe me, they are. I can feel it. He is an astute businessman, but an honest one. He'll keep his side of the deal, believe me Asha has a happy life ahead."

That night, when the boys were in bed, and Pappaji in his easy chair, the girls laughed all over again as Bina-Ma told them of Sethji's brilliant sleight-of-hand. She herself had halved the share by ensuring that the overall weight of gold in each half was about the same, but Sethji had rearranged Asha's share of her mother's jewelry so that it was much heavier than the other half; and since his own jeweler was going to replicate the rest, the Seth had made sure the gold in the new jewelry would be much more than in her mother's. Smart man, *beti*, smart family you are getting into.

Pappaji, who thought he would pretend he did not hear, was needled into entering the conversation. "And where do you think the money is to come from?"

"Not from a *class two* civil servant's salary, for sure," Bina-Ma laughed. "The girls' mother, good woman, seems to have managed the house far better than I, that she saved enough from your civil servant's salary to build up a nest-egg."

"She came with all that jewelry," Pappaji said gruffly, remembering how little he had given her of gifts or time.

"I don't mean that, but this," and Bina-Ma opened the little pouch that always hung from her waist, and let two small bars of raw gold peek out. "Aren't you glad I didn't show them these, else he would have talked you out of these two ingots as well. I don't know if there is enough gold here to make a complete set, you just might have to dip into your Provident Fund..."

"My Provident Fund is just that—for our retirement, and not to be frittered away on dowry"—he spat out the forbidden word. "Thank God we need to make only Asha's half now."

"Oh no," Bina-Ma said, "we have to make both at the same time. Both girls must have an equal share. And moreover, Asha's part of her mother's treasures will go with her and we'll forget what their patterns are by the time our little Namita gets married. Lalaji, sharif Lalaji, you will just have to borrow the money from somewhere. But believe me, Asha will be happy."

And indeed she was. Asha's in-laws were good people, and they treated her with love. And she did her part too. She took over a great many responsibilities from her mother-in-law without ever making the old lady feel the she was not every inch a good tyrannical mistress of the house. Within three years, she bore two children in the right order, a son first and then a daughter, and everyone approved her every step. Except Pappaji. When she became pregnant within six months of the wedding, he swore he wouldn't get Namita married off until she was twenty-one. "It was different with us," he said, knowing his women would start a spell of laughter, "If we had waited, why, Asha might have ended up with a brother young enough to be her son."

Pappaji did wait till Namita was twenty-one. She got her B.A. degree before he embarked on a search for his second son-in-law. She enrolled for a Master's degree while they waited for a suitable match. Then came this contact from another country, one Tarun Neggill, who lived in a place called Winnipeg in Canada, and earned a princely salary of 45,000 rupees a month. Suddenly everything moved very fast. There were long distance conversations, followed by a long distance engagement for which the young man's uncle and aunt came as proxy, and the wedding date was fixed. Pappaji said Tarun's family had left all arrangements to them; such decent people, he said, they wanted nothing. Just do whatever you can for your daughter, they said, we make no demands.

This time, Bina-Ma was out of her depth; she did not know how to deal with people long distance; she was one of those who still felt uneasy speaking on the telephone. She kept saying she wished their dear little *beti* did not have to go so far away. But, and she could see it for herself, their little *beti* was quite an independent young woman now, and she was earning her own living, teaching at a school nearby, and going to the School of Music in the evenings. She came home every payday with two saris, in the latest design, for herself and for Bina-Ma; they still did many things together, including music, but Bina-Ma knew things were beyond her now. Canada, so far away, why did anyone want to go so far away? she asked time and again. She herself had never wanted anything other than this patch of land, this river, this peacock farm she had grown to love, and all her children and grandchildren close to her.

Bina-Ma knew, Namita thought, in her deep intuitive way Bina-Ma must have known something which she could not articulate, dared not articulate because of her simple belief that if one said out aloud anything bad, it would come to pass. She, who had so cleverly worked their way out of the tangle of Asha's dowry to everyone's satisfaction, could not do anything for Namita. Because everything bad started only much later. After Tarun had left to return to Canada, taking her virginity and heart with him in a whirlwind of wedding and reception and honeymoon. His parents stayed on, visiting one relative after another. That is when trouble started, as Namita later found out.

A month after her arrival, Menaka took up a temporary job at one of the stores run by a friend. The next two weeks were heavenly for Namita. Tarun came home for very long lunch-breaks, and while his parents took their nap, the two of them slipped upstairs and made love on the queen-size bed and talked in whispers. It was then that he told her of where the dowry problem had started. He explained that the relatives were to blame, asking his parents what the new daughter-in-law had brought as dahej (dowry) and filling them with dissatisfaction. Then it had mounted up, with her father fuming to a go-between about deceit and hypocrisy. No doubt the go-between had exaggerated everything, Tarun agreed, but his parents' izzat was hurt, badly hurt. They don't want you here, he had said, because they feel insulted that your father did not yield an inch, but don't worry, we just have to wait till they take to you.

Tarun's parents sent between-the-lines messages through go-betweens that they wanted a cash settlement. Just what was traditional, they maintained. Their family's airfare, for example; five of them had flown at their own expense from Canada at high season fare, and they had assumed, so said the middle-men, that Pappaji would reimburse their fare. And then the clothes for family members; they had explicitly said they did not want any because Indian clothes and fashions were unsuited for Canada, but they had implicitly assumed that Pappaji would give them cash instead, three suits for the men at five hundred dollars each. And the wedding itself—what a small affair it had been, certainly not what they had assumed an old established Jaipur family would provide for them and their guests. But what was past was past. Never mind. But they did expect a cash settlement, ten *lakhs* surely was not unreasonable for a foreign-based son-in-law. There were minor confrontations, and then a major one just before they returned to Canada.

Two days after Canada Day, Namita saw the morning newspaper on the table and picked it up. She turned to the Business Section. One Indian rupee equals .034 cents, she read. She calculated: Thirty rupees equals a dollar, three thousand rupees equals a hundred dollars; one hundred thousand rupees equals three thousand three hundred and thirty three dollars; ten lakh rupees equals thirty three thousand dollars. One or two years' salary for Tarun, but fifteen, maybe twenty years gross salary for her father. A cup of coffee cost a dollar, may be more. Thirty rupees for a cup of coffee. Why would anyone ruin a woman's life for a mere year's salary? She could earn that much money easily, not in a year may be, but in three years; she would work it out with Tarun when he called. Together they could give them what they wanted—thirty three thousand plus interest—and they could cut themselves free. Together they could do anything they set their mind to in this country. O Canada, our home and native land. How proudly Robby had stood with hand on his chest and belted out the anthem, how gleefully Deena had beaten her hands on Rick's head to the drumbeats and crackers of last night. O Canada, our home and native land. My children's home and native land. Namita clenched her fist determinedly. Here I shall stay and here my children will be born. I have to be patient. I must not phone him. I must wait.

The next day, Tarun phoned. The Receptionist said she would give Namita the message. She added that he should try again in a few minutes.

Namita was paged, even though she was right there within sight of the Receptionist, who knew she was there. Namita had been told that was the system. She would be paged if anyone by chance came in person to ask for her. She should not come to the lounge. She would be given a message if anyone called, and it was her decision whether or not she called back. If, however, she gave them a specific request with a specific name that she should be called to the phone if that person called, then she should come to the phone when paged. She had given Tarun's name and said she would want to speak to him when he called.

She ran up and was asked to wait till he called again. "What if he didn't?" she was frantic. He called and she eagerly grabbed the receiver.

"How long will you be there?" was his first question. "I have to meet you. Did you get the papers?" He spoke in Hindi, as they always did.

"What papers? The divorce papers? They are a terrible mistake, aren't they? When did you come back? When can you come?"

"Whom have you talked to?"

"So many different people; all so sweet; everyone is so helpful…"

"Like whom have you talked to? Counselors? Lawyers?"

"I am supposed to meet one tomorrow."

"A lawyer?"

"Yes, a Legal Aid lawyer, they said."

"Don't tell him anything till you hear from me."

"It was all a mistake, isn't it?"

"Yes, it was all a mistake. I'll call back tomorrow. I am calling from work. I have to run."

Tarun ran to his lawyer. His lawyer's office was in the basement of a building which housed a Chinese restaurant, a Caribbean grocery and a used-furniture warehouse of sorts. The steps to the basement were littered with Styrofoam plates and cups. The smell of sauce and french-fries assailed one's nose. He knocked on the door and entered. Chalak Singh was in his usual pose—legs on table, cigarette in hand. His turban lay on the side table. The basement was hot; a table fan revolved lazily. "Tarun Sahib, come in, come in, what can I do for you?"

"You didn't tell me she would get a lawyer so fast."

"Calm down, Tarun Sahib, here, let me open a Cola for you." He got up, went to the refrigerator and took out two cans of pop.

"What are you panicking about? Everything is going according to schedule isn't it? One thing you have to do, my friend, and that is to get someone to sign an affidavit that you shared an apartment with him from February 4 to June 30, that is, from the day she phoned you from Jaipur to say she was on her way till the day after she left your house. If you can find someone, fine, otherwise I can line up a friend who owes me big time, but it should be done well before the hearing, okay? It may not be needed, but it is better to play safe and have proof that the two of you have lived at two separate addresses.

He took out his copy of the Petition, and scanned it for his notes. "Another point, Bhai, you have to do a little mouth work about what you have claimed. Time to start the ball rolling—tell a few friends about how let down you feel that she's cheated on you even before landing here. Make up a story and stick to it. No need for details, but always repeat the same story. Choose the right people—at your workplace, get your immediate supervisor. I don't have to tell you how to go about it, a bit of a preamble apologizing for bringing personal matters to him and then, with due hesitation, about the arranged marriage, the long delay in her arrival, and then you let drop about her adultery, never anything specific. Same with your friends at the temple, and at the community college course you are taking. Always the same story."

He checked off a couple of points on another sheet in the folder. "And never forget that the story you tell now must tally with what you've said here—a year and a half ago, in March, and you remember the date because it was your birthday, she called you from India and said she was not planning to join you; that takes care of the one-year clause, and mental cruelty number one; imagine how depressed it made you to get that kind of birthday present. But you took it like the strong man you are, and wished her well. Next thing you know she calls you from Toronto last February, when you were visiting your parents—never forget that your moved out to your friend's apartment the day she phoned from Jaipur—and she taunts you that she had made good use of the sponsorship papers and was in Canada but had no plan to join you in Winnipeg—that goes with the mental cruelty claim you've got here," he tapped the Petition. "And then, five days later she landed at your parents' doorstep, just like that, and refused to leave."

"But what if I trip on cross-examination? You never said she would get a lawyer this fast."

"Calm down, calm down. Here," he pushed a box of tissues and raised the fan speed by a notch. "Cross examination—you are right, you will trip, and so here is the solution—NO cross examination. Simple, very simple. Now listen carefully. You have to meet her, talk to her. Remember the main story—your parents are the bad guys. You have to persuade her that if she would play along for a while, and not contest the divorce, you can get together soon. If she contests it, she will never see you again. Get it?—promise her everything—tell her she must play along and let the divorce go through and all will be well—you'll be in her bed before she turns around; you will live your secret life with her and remarry her good and proper as soon as your parents go on their next visit to India. She is not to contest the divorce. That is all she needs to tell her lawyer. She must stand fast on that. No contesting."

Tarun mopped his face. "I have to get back to work." He rushed out.

Chalak Singh placed his feet back on the table and took out a cigarette. "Tarun," he wrote in his appointment book against the date, "two hours consultation, add to Neggill file." A secretary, who came in for a few hours twice each week, would take care of making the proper entries on the proper forms and vouchers.

He opened the second drawer of his desk and poured himself a shot of whiskey. He told himself he should go after some richer cases, may be get some decent office space, team up with someone else; but all that meant more overheads, more paperwork. Now he netted ninety percent of whatever he made. He liked it this way. He got cash for small favors, from taxi drivers, small businessmen who ran small shops in run-down areas of town, most of them from within the community, a few from outside, like Chan-Lee upstairs, who got into trouble time to time from Health Inspectors. Time to warn him about the garbage stink. Another hundred bucks billed for timely advice. Which Lee would not heed, and then there would be more paper work and more income. No one could blame him of not advising his clients to take preventative measures against possible infringements. But he really should get around to more lucrative deals. If only he could get start a pipeline on marriages of convenience with divorcees, like this Namita once this was over, wouldn't she be happy to sponsor someone for hard cash? but women were generally too unco-operative. Once they tasted freedom, they held our men in contempt, he thought, and spat out the idea. Women, ugh, it was well he kept his own on short leash.

Shayna came with the lawyer that afternoon, made the introductions and left. The lawyer was a tall thin man, balding and weary looking. "Everything is okay," Namita told him. "My husband phoned this morning and said it was all a mistake."

He patiently explained that the paper work had to be done. He advised her to contest the petition, and to ask for spousal support. They were standard procedures; he would go over it step by step, but first he needed to ask some questions. He opened the file Shayna had given him. It contained a copy of the Petition. She tried to snatch it out of the file. How had it gotten there from her bag? she wanted to know. Shayna had made a copy of it, didn't she remember giving her papers to Shayna so they could help her?

She didn't need their help. Her husband had phoned that morning. "Ms Neggill," the lawyer said, "we are here to help you. You are new to Canada, but we are not. Just hear me out."

"My husband told me I should not speak to anyone until he called me again."

"Ms Neggill."

"He told me not to speak to anyone."

The lawyer closed his file. "Ms Neggill, you need help. Keep in touch through Shayna."

Shayna came again the next morning. She had all the papers for income assistance, and she went through each line with Namita, making sure she filled it out correctly. Seeing that Namita was not opening up, she ventured, "The lawyer spoke to me this morning."

"I don't need him. I told you, my husband is coming soon, maybe this evening."

Shayna spoke softly and slowly, telling her about the difference between emotions and the law. No matter what her husband said or did now, the legal point was that he had sued for divorce. It would always be her word against his, and he had people to vouch for anything he wanted. Perhaps it would be a good idea, she suggested, that Namita get some contact with her own ethno-community. The thought had never occurred to her. Now that Shayna had put it into her head, Namita was excited. Of course, she knew where she could go, the temple, the gurudwara, Indian spice stores, restaurants, dozens of places where she could find people from India. Why had it never struck her? But then, where was the need? Tarun had phoned and said it was all a mistake.

He had never taken her to the temple. Every Sunday, her father-in-law went with one of his sons, usually Tarun, for Bhaiyan had no patience to sit cross-legged on the floor for two hours. At dinner, they spoke about community news and who was getting married when, who was going to India when and for how long. Menaka and the mother soaked up every bit of gossip, and relayed it on the phone to their friends, but it seemed to be the custom of the house that women did not go to the temple.

The next day, Krista came to her at the breakfast table. It had been arranged to transfer Namita to another shelter. Now that the paper work was underway, Namita could leave Bournedaya House, and enter the Women's Shelter run by the Salvation Army. Namita panicked. I can't go, I have to stay, she started crying. Thinking she had got attached to the Counselors, Krista described the Shelter. Everything would be the same as here, three meals a day, counselors to help. It was a much larger place, she would get a bus pass, there would be people to tell her how to get around, she would be fine, absolutely fine, girl, don't you worry.

But then Namita told her why she could not leave yet—her husband had said she should not do anything until he called her, and so she had to stay, had to.

Krista gave up. Okay, she said, you can stay till he calls, but do be careful with him.

"He is not like that," Namita said, thinking to herself these people would never know how strongly rooted their culture was, how different Tarun was from people here.

Tarun phoned the next morning. He said he would come around that evening. He asked for the address. Coached by Krista that she should not give the address to anyone, but that she could choose Eaton's Place as a meeting point, she told him she would meet him at the bus stop on Carlton near Eaton Place, and asked him to name a time. He promised everything would be all right, as long as she stayed where she was and did not speak to anyone.

"He is coming," she ran to Krista. "He said he is coming. Can I go with him?"

"We are a safe house, not a prison," Krista said. "We can't hold you here if you wish to go." She was tired. She knew she was being terse, but she was giving up on this woman. It was no use. One couldn't help anyone who did not want to be helped. If only one could give them a couple of slaps and force them to shape up, she thought. Krista was doubly tired because Alina had gone back to her husband. If Alina did not have the good sense to know what she should do after her experience of two years, why would this young woman? May be what she said was true, that his family was pressuring him. What a wimp, she thought, what an anemic wimp if he couldn't stand up to his bully of a brother and father. Krista felt very tired. It was like bashing one's head against a brick wall. If even just one out of ten women would just get out of the cycle, even one of every twenty, fifty. If it weren't for the children, she wouldn't be here day after day. Volunteers had often left, saying they couldn't take the suffering of the children. But for Krista, children were her raison d'etre. Oh god, we insist on licenses for sitting behind the wheel of a car; why don't we have mandatory revocation of parenthood licenses.

Chapter Three

It was the fourth weekend of July. Namita was in the Salvation Army residence. It had been a traumatic experience—the faces of the men, many disabled, many with bloodshot hung-over eyes, ghoulish sights wherever she turned—of men and women who looked, walked, talked differently. She could not figure out who was disabled, who was drunk or drugged, though she was told no one who got drunk could get back at night. The women's floor was full of young women. Namita felt a chill running up and down her spine when she saw them, their real faces hidden beneath layers and layers of heavy make-up. Every morning everyone was woken up at some unearthly hour and asked to sign that they were in. Donuts and pastries were available in plenty, and there was a lot to eat at every meal, though all she could safely eat was the salad and bread rolls, which she figured had no meat of any kind. She ate more of donuts than of anything else.

Tarun came every day and took her out for a drive. He parked at odd places, and they groped and kissed and made out in a frenzy. He did not speak much, and when he did, it was to say all would be well as long as she let her lawyer allow the divorce to go through without making any demands for herself. He would take care of her. As long as she kept their life a secret from the family, all would be well. He dropped her off at the corner of Henry and Main every day, and she walked back in a daze of pleasure and hope.

She told him of every new step she had taken each day—how her income assistance was in place, how the Housing Authority had given her the go ahead, how her résumé had been typed up by Shayna…. She never asked him about his stated reasons for filing those papers—how could he have thought for a moment she would have gone with any other man, and what did he mean by mental cruelty? She did not ask him anything. She just lapped up the moments of togetherness and thought of them all night and all day until he came again.

Then he stopped coming. One day, she received papers from the Court. The divorce had been granted. There was no provision for spousal support. She had thirty days to appeal. She called Shayna, who called the Legal Aid lawyer. As Namita had instructed him, he had not contested. There was no provision for spousal support. "But that is not what I meant," she said, no contesting did not mean she wanted no spousal support.

Another lawyer was assigned to her. He filed for support. Tarun came again and took her for a drive. He raged and ranted. How dare she appeal and ask for spousal support? He would never come again, never. Because if he did, he just might break every bone in her body. He'd had it. He was through.

She phoned her new lawyer next day in tears and told him of how her husband had threatened her. Shayna accompanied her to his office and she signed her complaint. Then all hell broke loose. Tarun appeared, made her get into his car, drove her out to the highway, stopped the car and raged at her. How dare she lie to her lawyer about him threatening her; he would never come again, never as long as he lived, she was dead to him and he to her. She begged and cried, cried and begged, she'd do anything as long as he promised he would come every day. He made her write to her lawyer that she had never complained to him about her husband, that there was some serious lapse of communication. Yes, she wanted reconciliation between her husband and herself. But and this is important, he had never threatened her in any way, why had the lawyer so misunderstood her position? She wrote what he dictated, signed it and gave it to him.

Next day, she called the lawyer and repeated all that she had written. She also said she had met her husband the previous evening and that he had been very angry and said he would never see her again if she did not contact her lawyer, and that she could not live without his daily visit. The lawyer could not figure out what she really wanted.

Shayna met with the Krista for a consultation. Krista knew just what was happening—the same see-saw movement that she had seen a thousand times in a hundred different women, but there was nothing concrete they could use. It was his word against hers, and the court had already accepted that she had been adulterous and cruel.

Namita started getting excited with the prospect of a place of her own. She was getting adept at finding her way around the city on buses, at going to shopping malls and leaving her résumé at every store. She had been at the shelter for two weeks, and now its familiarity was comforting. She greeted the disabled men by name, joked with the seeming-derelicts who opened the door for her, kept out of the way of the young women on her floor, volunteered around the dining room and lounge.

It was Sunday. Janet, at the Reception Desk, said there would be a service at the Chapel at ten o'clock, and she'd be glad to take Namita if she felt like it. Namita felt suddenly awake. Why had she not thought of it before? She would go to the temple. Her suitcases had been stored in the office, and she thought she would take a salwar-suit out for the temple. But then she decided her everyday clothes were good enough. She had washed her clothes the previous evening. One needed clean clothes for the temple; one did not need Indian outfits. But she finally decided to go with a salwar-suit. After all there would be older women and men. After all, she had never worn jeans back home. She imagined what Pappaji might say.

She went to Janet and said with some excitement, "I have to find out how to get to 854 Ellice." Janet smiled and said, "Sure, and you know how, right?" Jan knew when to channel people to be independent. She gestured towards the transit number that was on the bulletin board. "986-5700," Namita said. "You're getting there, Namita," Janet said.

Namita dialed 986-5700. "Please, how do I get from Main and Henry to 854 Ellice?" she asked, while Janet nodded approval.

"Take 18 going south to Garry and Graham, and then 14 going west. 14 goes all the way on Ellice. Do you know the cross street?"

"No, but you've been helpful. Thank you."

Each phone conversation boosted her self-confidence. "Please" at the beginning of every sentence, "thank you" at the end. The rule was so simple. If she could just work on her accent. She seemed to stress the wrong part of words; she knew she was doing it wrong, but couldn't figure out what was right for each different word. Even simple words like "adult." Who would have thought it was "A-dult" with a long wide Ah instead of the stress being on the "dul" as she had thought all these years? She watched television all day, trying to watch the women's mouths as they spoke. When she told that to Janet one day, Janet nodded approvingly, and suggested she watch the News channel if she really wanted to learn the accent. But, of course, the lounge TV was seldom on the News Channel.

Namita had another wash, and checked that the bus pass was in her handbag, that she carried close to her at all times even though she now felt much safer about the safety of the locker in her room. Then she came down, and said good-bye to Janet. "Have a good day," Tim hobbled ahead of her to open the door. "Thank you, Tim," and he gave her a high five. On the first day he did it, she had instinctively shrunk away from his wasted hand, that she associated with leprosy, that highly infectious disease so highly visible everywhere in India; even now, she was not wholly at ease with Down's Syndrome and Thalidomide victims, of whom there were two, who were in the lounge most days, but now she saw them as people, with names and faces. Tim, Jon, Barry, Brandon. Rehab, Stabilization Unit, Detox, Drunk Tank. Her vocabulary grew every day, and her self-confidence.

"You've come a long way, baby," was Counselor Dorothy's favorite phrase. Namita repeated it to herself many times each day. Number 18 took its time coming. By now, she took bus rides in stride. Always start the sentence with "Excuse me."

"Excuse me, could you please tell me where I get off for Garry and Graham?"

"That's Winnipeg Square you're looking for, ma'am?"

"I need to transfer to 14."

"Yep, Winnipeg Square it is. Sure will."

It was a bright sunny day, not a cloud in the sky. Oh the world was so beautiful. Number 14 took an even longer time coming. Sundays, Janet had said, Sundays are real slow.

"Excuse me, could you please tell me where I get off for 854 Ellice?"

"Should be past Arlington, I'd guess."

"It is the Hindu Temple."

"Okie, right, no problem."

Namita always stood behind the driver, even if the bus was empty. In the last day or two, she had felt safe enough to sit on the seat behind him, if there was a seat.

"Your stop next."

"Thank you. Have a good day," she said.

"You take care," he said.

The temple. Her heart raced. She was entering the temple. She bowed; she touched the steps with her fingers and raised her fingers to her forehead. The sound of sacred music floated to her ears as someone opened the double doors and entered ahead of her. She could see two women taking off their coats and she followed them. She took off her shoes, went in after them into the washroom, washed her hands, and followed them into the prayer hall, which was half full, it being past eleven o'clock. Holy holy holy space.

She was transported into it; the altar was a kaleidoscope of lights and tinsel streamers; she closed her eyes and let the music sink into her being. She took her seat at the side, almost at the foot of the altar of the Divine Mother. The Mother sat on her tiger in a resplendent glow of mini-lights that revolved first in one direction, then in another, the gold circles on her red sari glimmered, her bare sword was raised, the large diamonds on her crown flashed. Glory glory glory Durga Mata, divine mother supreme. Namita closed her eyes and knew she was home at last. Glory glory glory.

People kept coming, in ones and twos. Namita closed her eyes, and let the music sink in. Soon, her thinking process came alive again, and she recognized that some of the singers were rather off-key. She rebuked herself. Too much knowledge of music; that was her problem. She would not think, only feel. She closed her eyes.

"Before we have Prasad distribution, we have announcements. It is our custom to give a special welcome to first time visitors. Please identify yourselves so we can greet you." The young woman next to Namita nudged her, but Namita only smiled. "Next time," she whispered, "may be next time."

"You are invited to join the Preeti Bhoj downstairs…." Everyone rose and the line to the basement started forming.

"That is the best part," said the older woman next to her, winking. "You are new, I see. What is your name?"

"Namita."

"Speak Hindi?"

"Yes, I'm from Jaipur."

The other woman immediately switched to Hindi. She wanted to know Namita's full name, which Namita evaded; whether she was married or single, married; whether she had children, no not yet; whether she worked in an office, she was still looking for a job; where did she live? north of downtown; so how long had she been here? five months; what was her husband's line of work? what did do?

He's abandoned me. That would have been a proper reply, but Namita knew it was time to run; she said, "Excuse me," and stepped out of the line. The young woman who had nudged her earlier, and had watched her as she was being interrogated, motioned to her to join in front of her.

"My turn to grill," she said with a laugh. "My name is Charu," she said, "what is yours?"

"Namita."

"New to Winnipeg?"

"Yes, you been here long?"

"Like, six years."

"Like it?"

"Yeah. As nice a place as any. You?"

"Yeah. I've never seen a friendlier place. Please, thank you, have a good day, take care, keep well. People have been so overwhelming in their kindness."

"Really? Are we talking about the same place?"

"Don't you think so?"

"Dunno. Like, do they really mean it? Or is it just a lip thing?"

"Really. People have been so wonderful."

Charu shrugged. "Guess you've been lucky."

"Come every Sunday?" Namita asked.

"Whenever I can. By yourself?"

"Yeah. You?"

"Me too. And glad to be."

Namita looked at her, and suddenly felt herself smiling.

"You too, hnh?" she said, probing cautiously.

"You too, no!!" surprised and pleased. "I thought so when you slipped out of that interrogation in a hurry, but wasn't sure. You don't have to answer everyone's questions, you know."

"But how? I guess I have to learn how to dodge the questions without turning people off."

"You'll learn."

"Lovely altars."

"Too glitzy for my taste, but I guess it's okay."

"He never brought me here," Namita said.

"Mine neither, not after the first year anyway. Pigs."

Both smiled even more broadly at each other.

"This is just so good. Imagine running into you, that the very first person I run into should be you." Namita said.

Charu stepped out of the line and drew her off too. They moved back into the center of the hall "We can talk now. Downstairs it is too noisy. So where did you find your helpful people?

Namita did not want to open up that widely yet. She did not answer.

Charu nodded. "Is okay. Time enough." She led the way to rejoin the line. "Just that I sure didn't find any here, and I wanted to know how and where you found any. See them? All these ladies, not one has any real empathy. Men are like that, they said. They'll come around, they said. Don't wash dirty linen in public—that's their favorite line. Which makes me wonder how many of them are putting up with horse manure and not letting on."

"Not one will help?"

"Not that I know of."

"I came here thinking I'd get some help from someone who'd understand our culture."

"Wrong place. But there are some out there, don't let me crush your optimism. Some of our women are in every area, Social Work, Employment Counseling, ESL, University; good work they do too, but they don't often come to temples. There is Madhu Aunty who works for Psychiatric Services; there is Prem Aunty who works for Family Services; and Maru, who is on all kinds of women's organizations. I could give you a whole list of names, if you wish, and of some helpful ones who go to the gurudwara. But these women who really care come to the temple only once in a long while. This place is for gossip and good food."

"You are cynical."

"Like, when he raped me three times one night when I was six months pregnant, and I miscarried, know what one of these ladies said, 'Don't mind it, you'll conceive again.' You pour out your heart to them, but do they see or feel anything?"

"We shouldn't be talking such things here."

"God doesn't mind. He knows it already, remember."

They stopped whispering as the line narrowed down the basement stairs. They joined the line and went down to the basement. The food was indeed, good. And for Namita, after four weeks of donuts, it was manna from heaven.

They clasped hands before taking leave of each other. It had been wonderful, but it was not yet the time to exchange phone numbers or to say one didn't have a phone.

"Downtown," Namita had said, as her first choice when filling out the Housing Form. She got a wide choice of addresses. Downtown is the easiest, Shayna said, slum landlords a-plenty. Shayna helped her sort through the Accommodations list and came up with four addresses. She was sorry she couldn't come with Namita, but she gave her all the pointers she could and promised she'd advise her once Namita narrowed the four to two.

One was a small house on the corner of Sargent and a small street, where the owner wanted to rent out one of the two rooms on the top floor; the other was a three-storied apartment block with four suites on each floor, two houses from Isabel and three blocks from Portage Avenue. The vacant unit was on the second floor; an efficiency suite with a separate kitchenette, a built-in dining nook and a very large walk-in closet. Shayna pointed out the plus/minus of both places. The home-owner seemed friendly and she said the tenant could use the laundry downstairs and her phone as long as it was for local calls; but she was old, the stairs creaked, and there was only one front door. The apartment was as crumbly looking, and overlooked a garbage bin, one had to take one's laundry to the Laundromat, and had to pay for telephone service, but the caretaker was a strong young man who lived in the building, and he seemed a helpful guy.

They decided on the apartment.

Sandy Ketts was one of the volunteers at the Shelter. He was a full time student at the University of Winnipeg, in his graduating year, but even so, he came three times a week to the Shelter, just as he had for the last three years. He was a strapping Adonis of a young man—tall and chocolate brown, with a set of teeth one could die for, as Namita heard one of the young women say to another. Whenever Namita heard a word or phrase that attracted her, she jotted it down on a calendar with scenes of Taj Mahal that a cousin had given her before she left Jaipur. She had written only two entries in it. On February 6th, she had entered: "Left Jaipur for Delhi with Pappaji and Bina-Ma. On Feb.10th she had written, "Writing this in the waiting area of Indira Gandhi International Airport. Left Chachaji's flat at midnight by taxi with Pappaji and Bina-Ma. Checked in at 1:30 a.m. Another two hours to go. Can't believe I am really on my way."

Since coming to this shelter, she wrote something every day. She wrote in tiny letters, about people she had talked to each day. Often she wrote phrases she had heard and liked. "Teeth one could die for," had a nice ring to it. Tarun has hair one could die for, she practised saying it; indeed he did, a shock of black thick hair that one could run one's fingers through. "Eat crow," she had heard someone else say at breakfast. It took her a long while to figure out even the words, let alone the meaning of that phrase, and then only when Janet had explained it.

Sandy was the most wonderful guy she had seen among all the wonderful people she had had the good fortune of meeting during the last four weeks. She had a whole list of his repartees on her calendar diary. He was so handsome, the middle-aged women in the shelter had to say it, "How can such a good-looker be so patient too?" and he had a different answer each time.

"Lot of hard work, Ma'am, I do nothing but practise patience from midnight to three a.m. every night."

"Not easy, Ma'am, takes me thirty minutes four times a day to floss my teeth,"

"Take it from me, Ma'am, it is hard work being so handsome."

He addressed all women as "Ma'am," just as Krista said "Girl." Krista had explained that people's need for anonymity had something to do with her habit. Janet made it a point to call everyone by her first name.

Namita wrote down all these thoughts and trivia in the minutest possible letters under March and April pages of her calendar, noting the actual date of the entry first; and now she was into the end of April. She wrote what someone else said of Sandy the previous evening: "one gorgeous hunk of flesh."

She repeated the words to him this morning. "I am learning," she said, "two phrases every day, and I'll soon be Canadian, eh?"

He smiled. "Sally Hemmings," he said. "Add that for today even if it isn't a Canadian eh phrase. What happens when the beauty of Africa gets mixed with the skin color of Europe."

"Your mother?" she asked.

"I guess there's no reason you should know her," he said. "She was President Jefferson's slave lady-love."

She told Sandy of her decision to take the apartment instead of the room in the house. "I'll be out of your hair in another week," she said. "Out of your hair" was another phrase that had fascinated her. Some of the young women on her floor had such wild hair, she could see little birds swarming in and out of their hair-dos.

"We'll miss you, but I am glad for you. You're really getting there, Namita, you can be proud of yourself."

"You've come a long way, baby," she said, repeating Dorothy's phrase because it sounded so good.

"Yes, Ma'am, you've come a long way."

Sandy wanted to know more about the move. Did she have any furniture? No. Well, he could help her get some basics from Goodwill or Value Village. Did she need a phone connection? Not yet. Don't wait too long, a phone is one's lifeline, you know. What about pots and pans? He could salvage some easily enough. And a bed, don't forget to sleep and breathe. He'd find out about getting a bed. He made a note of all these. He phoned the caretaker and said it would be good if she could move on Sunday instead of Monday, because he wasn't free to help on Monday.

Tarun phoned on Thursday. He had been away, he said. Slowly he got her talking, and soon she had told him everything, including where she was moving and when.

She was impatient for Sunday to come around again. She was at the temple by ten o'clock. There were hardly a handful of people. She helped them spread bed sheets on the carpets. Tarun came in, saw her, and quickly went downstairs. She went into the foyer. Among the men's coats, she recognized his, and put her face into it; a faint whiff of Player's No. 5 suffused her face. She looked among the footwear, and recognized his shoes. She bent and touched them with her fingers and raised her fingers to her forehead. Her first action had been deliberate, but her second had been reflexive. She had touched his shoes, she told herself. What was she doing? And yet, and yet, it had come so naturally…She was about to enter the prayer hall again when she noticed that Tarun was already there, seated in front of Siva's altar, on the men's side of the hall. She quickly walked backward and out, and took the other stairway to the basement.

Charu was there already. The two of them stood near the Library door. One of the women came out of the kitchen and addressed Charu in saccharine tones, "Charu, we have enough volunteers today; I think you can go upstairs." With equally cloying sweetness, Charu said, "Oh, aunty, do let us roll the chapattis so you can listen to the bhajans upstairs in peace." The woman turned away disapprovingly. Namita and Charu giggled discreetly. Charu said, "Some of them think the likes of us will pollute the food that is made for the offering." Another woman, on her way to the kitchen, said to Charu, "Could you please check if there are enough paper napkins for both Prasad and Lunch. If not, you know whom to ask for the key."

"Nice lady," Namita said.

"Yes, she's a nice person."

"Glad to hear that. You scared me the other day about the people here."

"May be I was thinking only of the nasty ones. Tell me again," Charu said, "did you really find white people helpful like you said last week?"

"Yes, don't you?"

"I am not so sure. They are probably well meaning but they are so ignorant, like they have no clue there is a world out there, no clue at all. They have such stupid ideas about India, the people I work with anyway, like, they assume I was in this deep hole because of an arranged marriage. So I have to tell them about it, if they stop long enough to listen, that it is not an oppressive thing at all, that ninety percent of Indo-Canadians they see were married that way and that most of them are probably happier than most couples here. That parents know what they are looking for—someone from a decent family, with the same background, language, food habits—stuff like that helps people get along. You never get to know a guy till you are married to him, and that is the simple truth whether you have an arranged marriage or not. I mean, there is this woman who works with me who lived with a guy for years, got married to him last year, and now they are getting divorced."

"I've never tried telling anyone anything. May be that is why I find them so nice. How can they understand anything about life in another country so far away? Mine was an arranged marriage, and as you say, most of them seem to work out all right."

"Awful truth is, mine wasn't quite one. I said no to the first two guys my parents had me meet, and then said yes to this jerk, even though he wasn't their choice once they met him. My Dad, especially, kept saying I was being carried away by looks. And I guess Dad was right. This guy had a kind of sex-appeal, like, and I insisted."

Namita thought again of Tarun, sitting upstairs. "Does you husband come here?"

"When we first came to Canada, we'd come together. But when things started going wrong, he would come once in a while and I once in a while, but never on the same day. Then, when word got around that he was beating me up, he stopped coming, and of course he didn't want me coming either. We dropped out of everything, temple, community parties, everything. It is an izzat thing, as you know. When a man has wronged a woman, whether his conscience ever troubles him or not, his status among his friends is affected by her very presence, and all he wants is for her to disappear from his social circle. But I didn't. So he left for Vancouver, and I got the house. A good enough deal, don't you think?"

A woman came to them, greeted Charu and turned to Namita. "You are a new face?"

"I am Namita."

"Namita what?"

"Give me also some job, please do."

The woman shrugged, smiled and went her way.

Namita whispered, "Oh I do so feel tempted to say I am Tarun's wife."

Charu raised her eyebrows. "Tarun? Wow. Be sure I am here when you spring that one on them. I'd love to see their faces."

"He comes often?"

"But of course, and ladies with daughters were after him ever since he came to Winnipeg five years ago."

"I've been married almost three years."

"Wow. I wonder how many people know he is married."

"Are you in the know of things? Like what people know and are talking about?

"No one talks anything personal to me, directly, as you can see, but gossip can be retrieved in many ways. Let's have some fun."

Charu went closer to the kitchen, and said to no one in particular, "I hear Menaka Neggill is expecting."

"High time, too. The way young women keep putting off starting on their families, pah," said one.

"So what is happening about Tarun?" said another. "Such a nice young man and to have such a terrible thing happening. Such bad luck. Poor man."

"What? What? Tell me, I haven't heard."

"Oh, it is all over the community. Poor boy, his wife was cheating on him all the time, and he is caught in a messy divorce."

"Really? I didn't even know he was married."

Namita felt nauseous. She left Charu and slipped upstairs. She stayed long enough to accept the sacred flame and fruits, and then hurried out. Charu, who had joined her, pressed her hand. "Stay a bit. Let's get out together. It is not true what I said about Menaka. I am sorry I started on anything." Namita returned the pressure but then rushed away.

"How could he? How could he spread such lies?"

Sandy was there at four o'clock as he had said. Janet was not on duty, but the usual crowd of men were there. They were so happy for her. Jon helped with the suitcases. Tim high fived her all the way to the car. Sandy drove her out to their bye-byes. Lovely people, Namita said, such lovely people.

"This is where I study," Sandy said, driving around the University block. "Nice place. You should think of taking a course at a time, may be. That would enable you to keep your Social Assistance, and still upgrade yourself." He looped back to Isabel and located her new home.

"I have put the bed in already," he said. "Buddy of mine has a van and I figured I'd do it when he could help. The caretaker is a nice guy."

The bed, pots and pans, a chair and a table, all were in place already. Sandy carried the suitcases upstairs, Namita apologizing for their weight, and he shrugging away her thanks. He then went back to the car, and brought in two bags of groceries. Namita expressed her surprise. She had not thought of anything at all. She had spent the afternoon crying.

Sandy put the milk and butter in the refrigerator, the cereal boxes tea, instant coffee, sugar, bread, all in the cabinet "That is all I could think of, he said, there is a convenience store just down the road, if you need more milk, you do have some money, right?"

He kept a flow of conversation, "Be sure to run the water a few minutes every morning before drinking it, some of these old places…Gee, we need to get a shower curtain for you…. See, you can even see Isabel if you squint from here, and the bus stop is just around the corner…I have got two blankets…. Look, here is the thermostat if you need to raise the heat…"

"Oh, Sandy," she kept saying, "Oh, Sandy, you are so kind I could cry."

"Oh no, Ma'am, you can't because I didn't remember to buy tissues."

He gave the apartment a once-over check, then led her out. He locked the door and gave her the key. "Tomorrow is the official opening. Wish I could be there to celebrate, but think of me. I have to rush off after dropping you at the shelter," he said.

"I forgot to tell Tim I am coming back for the night," Namita said, "and is he going to be puzzled when he sees me again."

"Remember, Ma'am, I am always only a shout away. Leave me a message any time you need any kind of help, any time of day, don't hesitate. Janet has my number but here is my card—made it on the computer, isn't it neat?"

❦   ❦   ❦

Namita opened the door to her apartment. Gone was the excitement of the previous evening. It was bare, the plaster peeling from the bathroom ceiling, the glass panes grimy with dust and cooking oil, the floor covered with a pathetic patchy carpet with cigarette holes.

She clutched the key in her hand, and went out for a walk. It was a warm day, and every house had children and adults with little on, splashing in wading pools, sitting under colorful umbrellas, pop cans in hand. The houses looked trim and painted on the outside, but were probably as run down inside as hers. Or may be not. "There is a difference between owner-lived houses and rentals," Shayna had said, "a huge difference." She felt better after an hour of walking, and went back. "Home," she said to herself. "A place of my own."

She bolted the door behind her, opened wide the window in the kitchen, and lay down. There was a knock on the door. She quickly sloshed her face, washed her mouth, and waited for Sandy's voice. Sandy, good Sandy, she thought. What was he bringing her now? The knock was repeated. It is me, he said. She gasped in excitement. Tarun. She opened the door. He came in, looked around, sat on the only chair in the room. He did not bother to take off his shoes for clearly the carpet did not warrant it.

"Nice location, very convenient, he said. "Just half a block from the bus route."

She did not say anything. He came to her, and led her to the bed. Despite herself, her body reflexively responded, and he could sense it. "I miss you," he said. "You looked so sweet yesterday, I wanted to hug you right then and there, but you disappeared so fast." And her body responded despite her uncertainty. His feet worked their way out of the shoes. And she had no control over her body.

"Can I come again?" he asked. "Please can I come again? I miss you so much."

"Any time you want," she heard herself saying. "Any time."

He came every evening all through the week, and even though her monthly began on Friday, she hid it from him, and received him and received him as though she were an ocean of waiting. During the morning, she brooded and cried, wondering where all this was leading to, but come afternoon she waited in a frenzy of desire. When the milk carton emptied, she bought a new one, and some fruits. She did not use the stove or cook anything. She was an ocean of desire, an ocean of waiting. She did not go to the temple that Sunday, for her temple promised to come to her every day. One evening, two or three weeks later, as they lay spent, she started thinking of all the things she meant to talk about every morning which she forgot all about every evening. She looked at her bare arms lying around his head of hair and marveled at how she had filled out in the last few weeks. "All those donuts have made me fill out, don't you think?" she said. "Soon I might even become as filled out as Menaka, and you would like that, wouldn't you?"

He rose. He propped her against the headboard with one hand and swung his other hand across her face. Back and across. Back and across. He punched her on her stomach. Then he left.

Namita knew now, beyond a doubt, that what she had hoped was merely her exaggerated fear and imagination about Menaka and Tarun was true.

He did not come again. She went to the temple on Friday evening and sat quietly for two hours until closing time. Then she went home and lay on her back. She went to the temple on Saturday afternoon, and sat quietly while the Tamil group had their prayer meeting in a language she could not understand. She went home and lay on her back. She went to the temple on Sunday morning and sat quietly near Durga Mata's altar long before anyone else came. She did not know what went through her mind. She was an ocean, but not waiting for anything. Water lapped against stones, wind sighed through waves.

He came again on Monday. She opened the door on hearing his voice because he was her husband, though her lawyer had called him "ex-husband." He forced himself on her. Then he slapped her. "I don't want you coming to the temple," he said. "Don't you dare come to the temple. Unless you want to get yourself killed one of these days." He deliberately took the duplicate key she had been given, that he knew was near the sugar bottle in the kitchen cabinet, and added it to his key-chain. Then he left.

She pulled the chair to the window, pulled the blanket around herself and sat, looking out. There was a narrow gap between the wall of the next block and the end of hers through which she could see the main road. She sat looking at the cars as they flitted through the gap. She slept for a while on the bed before taking up her vigil again at the window. Next morning, she sat there again, and started counting the cars, timing them on her watch. Each time, she waited till the second hand came to twelve before she started her count. There were sixteen cars one minute, fourteen another minute, twelve the next, only ten once. She jotted down the numbers on the *Lance* newspaper that was left under the door once a week. All night she heard someone pacing outside her room; there were occasional scratches on her door. She cowered in her bed and fell asleep early morning. Next day, there were twenty-two cars many of the times she was counting. Wednesday mornings the traffic is busy, she noted. She had been nibbling at the loaf of bread that had been in the refrigerator and sipping milk from the milk carton. Both were finished by Wednesday morning. She did not eat anything for the next fourteen hours. When she used the toilet, she did so with her eyes on the window. She did not shower. She did not want to be caught naked. She lay cowering in bed all night. Someone turned the lock but no one came in. There were footsteps outside her door all night. Someone scratched on the door several times.

In the early morning, she slept for a few hours.

She rose, brushed her teeth, and opened the refrigerator. It was empty except for a wilted cauliflower. She filled a glass with water and placed it near her bed. For the next twenty-four hours she lay in bed, tucking herself smaller and smaller under the blanket. Someone turned the lock but no one came in. Again there were footsteps outside her door all night. Someone scratched on the door several times.

As soon as it was morning, she pulled on her jeans, put on her coat over her nightshirt, clutched two quarters in one hand, Sandy's card in the other, rushed down to the 7-Eleven and dialed his number. His answering machine came on. "Sandy, Sandy," she sobbed, "please help, I need help, Sandy, please." She rushed back, expecting to have locked herself out, but the door was open. She looked into the bathroom and everywhere else to make sure there was no one else in the apartment, bolted the door, and cowered in bed all day.

There was a knock around five o'clock. "Namita, Ma'am, it is me, Sandy, Sandy Ketts, I picked up your call only now. I am so sorry, but I had to go to Carberry last night, and came back just now. I am so sorry I never thought to check my answering machine." She knew someone was at the door but could not quite hear. "Ma'am, Ms Neggill, it is me Sandy, you called me this morning," he repeated his phone number, "are you okay?" She wanted to go to the door but it was so far away.

After a moment, he spoke again, "Namita, Ma'am, I am going to get the caretaker to open the door, don't worry. It's Sandy."

She went to the door and unlocked the chain bolt and door, and fell against him. "Take me home," she said. He held her shivering body close against his own. "There, there," he said, stroking her as one would a wet squirrel. "There, there, everything is okay, you are safe."

He gathered a few of her needs, toothbrush, comb, some clothes, and through them into a 7-Eleven bag that lay on top of the kitchen counter. He wrapped her in the blanket and led her down to his car. On his cell phone he called the Shelter. "I am bringing Namita in. We need a room for her."

Chapter Four

"You can stay as long as you need to, Namita," Janet said. "It is too soon to be on your own."

"I have to leave some time, Janet."

"Take it a step at a time. Come back for the nights."

Namita took her advice. During the day, she lived in her apartment; she bought some grocery; she even ventured as far as Dino's and bought spices, wheat flour, lentils and a skillet. She ate cooked lunch; she washed up. Then she took bus trips until suppertime and returned to the Shelter. On Friday afternoon she was ready. "You need all the beds you can get weekends," she joked to Janet and Sandy.

Saturday morning Tarun was at the door. She was in the kitchen, putting a saucepan of water on the stove. They talked through the locked door in Hindi. He apologized for his behavior. He had been frantic, he said, at not finding her there all these days. Please, he begged, please let us talk. He did not know what devil had got into him; he must have been mad, he must have been out of his mind, to say and do what he had done. Please.

She let him in. He did look distraught, and she could feel her body responding, and he sensed it was so. He was cautious. There were now two chairs at the table, Shayna having given her a folding chair. He sat on one; she sat on the other, the table between them.

"We can work things out," he said. "They, my parents, are going to India this winter." He went on with family news—several weddings back home, they would be away for six months—he and Namita could work things out, if she would only be patient and accept his apologies. He berated himself again, expressed how devastated he was. Her mother had phoned again, he said.

"Again?"

She had phoned last month and Bhaiyan had said they were both away for the evening.

"Indeed."

And she had phoned two nights ago, about midnight, and Tarun had answered.

"And what was your explanation for me not being at home at midnight? Did you tell her I was away in my lover's arms?"

Tarun's arm rose threateningly but he controlled himself. "You know it was a necessary lie," he said. "I explained that right at the beginning."

"Of course," she said.

"I told her you would call her back." He looked around. "You still have no phone?"

"I don't have that kind of money. If I had got some spousal support, for instance," she was amazed at her own audacity in goading him.

His face got all puffed up. He is rather ugly, she thought with surprise.

He changed the topic. "You've set up the place well," he said.

"I am boiling some tea. May be you'd like some?"

He took it as an invitation. He moved forward. She rose and went to the kitchenette. He followed and stretched his hand to her shoulder, slowly stroking it as he drew closer. She lifted the saucepan and flung it straight on his arms and side; he staggered, and leaned his hand against the counter. She brought the empty saucepan bottom down on his hand.

"Get out of my house," she said. "And don't dare come back."

From the kitchen corner she took a dirty broomstick that had probably been there through six tenants, and shoved it against him, propelling him out the door. She fastened the chain bolt. She switched on the light and went to the kitchen to brew some fresh tea.

Then she left the tea untasted and cried, knowing all those deliberate actions were just that, actions deliberately gone through. "You have a long way to go, baby," she told herself, knowing she would gladly give all she had gained for a night in his arms.

Next morning she rose early, had a shower, took a twenty-dollar bill from her handbag, and went down to the 7-Eleven. She bought a tube of toothpaste and asked for all the change in quarters. She went to the phone booth and dialed her mother. When she heard Bina-Ma's voice, she thought she might cry, but she did not. Indeed, her voice came out light and happy, "Bina-Ma, how wonderful to hear your voice. How are you, how are Akhil, Nikhil, Pappaji, and is Asha pregnant again?" Bina said, "*Beti*, it is so comforting to hear your voice, we've been so worried, haven't heard from you in weeks, no letter, no phone call, we've been so worried."

"Of course, I am okay, I promise I'll write you a long letter soon, but now you give me the news. Tell me everything." It suddenly occurred to her that they might have written letters to her that had never reached her, stacked or thrown away by her father-in-law. She added, "Everything, even if you've written about it already."

Bina-Ma talked about each person at home and about friends. "Before I forget," she said, "did you get your Krishna intact?"

"What Krishna?"

Then her mother explained. Seth Govindji had come by some two-three months ago, and had noticed Namita's wooden Krishna standing on the bookshelf and had wanted to know why she had not taken it with her as she had promised she would. Bina-Ma had made excuses about her over-stuffed suitcases, and he had said he would send it to her properly packaged, and had taken down Namita's Winnipeg address. Ever since, he had been checking whether they had heard from her about its safe arrival. It should have reached by now, Bina-Ma said anxiously.

"It will, Ma, it will. I'll let you know the minute I lay my hands on it."

"It will bring you luck, *beti*, it is your own special Kanhaiya, your own special charm against the world. Carved with your name on it, that is what Seth Govindji said. You know his line."

"Yes, Ma, dane dane par likha hai khanewale ka naam…." (on every grain is written the name of the person for whom it was sown; millions are nourished, but the Giver is ever the same, Ram)

"But tell me, sweetheart, are you okay?"

"I went through some tough times, Ma, but I am fine now."

"I could feel it, sweetheart, I could feel it. But once Kanhaiya comes home, you will be fine."

"I have to go, now Ma. I love you all; I love you Ma. Take care."

Namita leaned against the booth and closed her eyes. Ma knew, had known all along, would always know and feel. Across the world she felt her mother's arms and pressed her face into the sweet smell of her milk-wet bodice where lay the ocean of life-giving *amrit*, now and forever hers to sip.

She needed to clear her head of all the chaos that assailed her from every side. She walked towards Portage. The morning traffic was building up. She walked quickly and reached the relatively quieter side of Memorial Boulevard. The fountains were playing. The grass was wet with the work of the automatic sprinklers of early morning. She kept to the paved paths. Come on, come on, she told herself. Quieten yourself so you can hear what Kanhaiya has to say.

As a child, her secret trysts in the Peacock Garden were with Krishna-Kanhaiya. She talked to him incessantly, tugged at all his many statues, of stone, of ceramic, of red clay, tweaked his stone ears, threatened to take away his flute, to break all the peacock feathers that she had picked up and tied with strings to his crown, unless he came pronto and talked to her, told her what to do about her homework, about mother's illness, about the lice on her head that she had picked up at school, about every problem she had. And he had always told her. Not in so many words, but in his own mischievous way he talked to her whenever she asked him anything.

The peacock garden. She knew why she had not phoned or written to her mother or anyone else back home. But why had she never gone to the peacock garden in all these days? And what insanity had made her leave her Kanhaiya behind just so she could cram her suitcases with more saris and trinkets? But now she had come to her senses. She felt herself growing light-hearted. "Okay, Kanhaiya, let us think this through. How do I get you home?"

She heard drumbeats. Not the drumbeats of the tabla to which she had danced at the Music School. But they transported her just the same. In one of the Fine Arts Theory course, she had learned about dances from all over the country, little snippets so they could study the common elements and compare the differences between the different dance styles. The Bharata Natyam dance they had studied was a Nataraja dance, and the song was in Tamil, about how the god of dance kept his promise to the sages and came in person to dance at the temple of Thillai. Their dance-master always translated the words, no matter in what language it was, so they could feel what they were dancing. He had given them a lecture on Siva iconography and made them repeat the mantra contained in the song: "Blessed is he who realizes that Thillai the eternal city is located in the heart of man."

The drumbeats were coming from a tepee set up in front of the Legislative Building, where a protest sit-in was being staged by native people. She remembered having seen it on the television news while at the Shelter.

"Okay, Kanhaiya, I think I get it. I have been a clod about our garden, thinking it was beyond me, forgetting it is right within me. Next, what do we do?"

She could phone Menaka and ask directly, but there was always the likelihood that Menaka would lie through her teeth. She could write to her mother-in-law, but even if the poor woman wanted to be on her side, she was under her husband's thumb and would never be allowed to write, or speak on the phone.

She should have asked Tarun if there were any letters for her, but now it was too late for that. It had felt good to beat the shit out of him—she savored the phrase she had picked up at the Shelter from one of the young women—but that was over and done with. No regrets. It was for the best. All that happened now on would be for the best. There was no other option. She had to go in person and retrieve her Krishna.

She went back to her apartment. As she reached her door, her neighbor's opened, and a young woman stepped out, carrying a toddler. "Hi," she said, "I am Wendy, and this is Tyler, and this is King." She put down the blue-eyed child, and locked the door. The little dog frisked around and scratched on the wall. The toddler ran up and down twice before she could check that she had locked the door. "Just knock if you need any help," she said. "I am always home. I have a daughter who goes to school. So I spend most of the day walking her to and back from school, morning, lunch hour and afternoon. But otherwise, I am home all day. Except when we figure we'll spend an hour at the playground before heading for school. Right, Tyler? Nice day, isn't it?"

Namita said, "Have a good day."

"You too."

Namita had a shower and took out a clean set of clothes. She combed her hair back and tied it in a neat ponytail. She looked around the apartment for a bag for her Kanhaiya when she got him, but couldn't find any. Instead her eyes alighted on a baseball bat that Sandy had brought for her the second time that she had come back. It was only black plastic, but appeared as though it was a real full size bat. "You never know when it might come handy," he had said, not quite wanting to feed her fears, but not wanting to leave her totally defenseless either. "A quick and decisive wallop can be very effective, even with a light weapon." Too bad she hadn't spotted the bat yesterday, she thought, it would have made it even easier to beat the shit out of Tarun. It had felt so good. May be she would take the bat after all.

She had already found out the bus routes for where she wanted to go. Bus pass and two loonies in her pocket, bat in hand, she set out. She overshot the bus stop on both the first bus and the connector, and had to wait to retrack each time. No matter, she had all afternoon for getting where she wanted to go. She thought of Krista and her ode of praise to the Transit System and how great it was to have a bus pass.

As she walked towards the in-laws' familiar and hated house, she felt a shiver of fear and anticipation. Kanhaiya, she said, my Kanhaiya, be with me now and always. She went up the steps and rang the bell. She hoped Menaka would open the door and not her father-in-law. No such luck. But may be it was lucky, because Menaka would have peeped through the peephole and told the others who it was and perhaps they would have refused to open the door. But of course, the macho pit bull didn't bother to peep. He was in his usual house clothes—striped pajamas and sleeveless sweater. He opened the door, and belligerently said, "What are you doing here?" She slipped under his elbow and entered the house. "How dare you," he dragged her by her sleeve. She wielded her bat to keep him off her, and walked in. She looked around the living room. Kanhaiya was not there. Where else would he be but in Menaka's room? She ran up the stairs, right into Menaka who stood with popped eyes. Downstairs, her mother-in-law had come out of her room and was trying to hold back her husband from chasing Namita up the stairs. Namita elbowed Menaka out of her way, walked into Menaka's room and sure enough, her Krishna was there, on the stereo stand. She swept him to herself, and started to walk down.

"How dare you," her father-in-law was saying, having pushed his wife away, "put that down at once."

"Just try stopping me," she said. He lunged at her as he climbed step by step. She backed up on to the upper landing, saw the canister vacuum cleaner sitting behind her, and pushed it down the stairs. The moment she pushed it, she realized it was a stupid thing to do, for now she would have to maneuver through the twisted hose and trailing cords when she ran down the stairs. But it turned out all right because the cord caught around the old man's feet as he raised his foot, and he fell. Even in her haste, she tried not to let her feet touch any part of his prone body, for it would never do to kick one's father in-law. Old beliefs die hard. One was supposed to touch the dust of his feet and ask for his blessing. He reached out to catch her by her ankles and she almost tripped.

"What a vindictive old man," she shouted in Hindi. "I just want to take what is mine and get out of this hell-hole," she said, shocking her mother-in-law. Menaka, stupid woman, blocked her way to the front door. It would feel so good to give her a whack with the bat, she thought, but resisted. She went into the kitchen, and whacked at the floor instead; it felt so good, she whacked at the storm window as well after she had opened the back door. She ran out, cradling her Krishna. Bhaiyan's second car was in the carport and she was sorely tempted to whack her plastic bat and hear the sweet tinkle of glass. But Kanhaiya would not like that, she thought as she looked at the treasure in the crook of her arm. She ran out, cradling her Krishna, and slowed down to a walk as she entered the back lane. She knew the old man would come chasing, but she also knew he would take some time to change into street clothes. She turned left, then right and left again, walking to the farther bus stop, so as to throw him off if and when he came out of the house. She stepped into the gas station convenience store near the bus stop, and smiled at the cashier. "Good day to you," she said. "Could I use the rest room, please?" He waved her in the right direction. Once in the washroom, where she had meant to leave the incriminating bat, she realized she had developed an attachment to it. She ran it under the faucet and wiped it off with toilet paper. She then came out, bought a chocolate bar and waited for the bus.

The bus going in the wrong direction came first. It was headed for Polo Park. She quickly crossed the street and got in. She made her way to the back and sat next to a teenager, even though there were many empty seats in the front.

"Nice day," she said. "I wonder if you could help me."

He grunted.

"Like, I am new to this country," she said.

He turned to her to give a quick look and grunted.

She continued seriously, "and I really would like to learn some strong street language."

He cleared his throat. "Hmm," he said sarcastically, "to go with the bat hnh?"

"No, the real thing, not plastic like this bat."

He grunted.

"Like, beat the shit out of you, you know, some real stuff."

"Kick butt," he said.

"Kick butt," she repeated.

"Shoot some crap," he said.

"Shoot some crap," she repeated.

"Asshole."

"Asshole."

None of them sounded as good as "beat the shit out of you," but no matter. There was time enough to learn. She took out the chocolate bar and offered it to him. "With thanks," she said.

"Hard to resist KitKat," he said and took it.

"Know what?" he said. "You gotta be born to street language. Don't sound the same coming from you."

"Maybe you're right," she said. "Guess I'll just have to be my prim and proper Paki self."

"Heh," he said, grinning, "you're okay. Have a good life. My stop is coming up."

She turned her legs sideways and let him slide out. "Thanks for everything," she said.

"You're okay," he said. "Take care. I'd get rid of the bat, though."

She sat back, cradling Kanhaiya in her arms and holding the bat between her knees. She went all the way to the Polo Park terminus, and got out to read the route-maps on the bus shelter to see what bus she could take to go where. The choice seemed limitless. She came back to the driver of the bus she'd been on and said, "Excuse me, could you help me figure out how I can get to Assiniboine Park?"

He told her.

"You've been very helpful," she said. "Have a wonderful day."

"Take care," he said.

Savitri

"Of course, I'm staying the night," Maru said. "How could you think otherwise even for a moment? Yes, I know Chander and the other men will take charge of everything; yes, I know Jayant and Krish will be here by the first possible flight; but Jyoti must go home; her children need her."

Maru interposed her interruptions as Savitri urged her to leave. Then she persuaded Jyoti to go home to her husband and children. She asked Chander, who was at the telephone making arrangements and informing relatives long distance, to drive Jyoti home. She watched them drive off. On his return, Chander would probably be at the phone half the night, informing and receiving calls. What a treasure he was, and had always been. God bless him and Chandrika. Wedding or funeral, they were always there to help.

Like the November sun that she had been watching from the hospital window, Sharad had slipped into the horizon quietly, quickly; one moment there the next moment not, while crimson gashes lazily played in the skyline behind the new apartment blocks on Chancellor Avenue.

She had taken Savitri home. Sharad and Savitri had been one of the first families to settle in Winnipeg, back in the sixties, and so the community network had been set in motion at once, with ready volunteers taking on tasks handed out by Chander. Visitors started coming within minutes of Maru and Savitri reaching home. The evening had been long and now, at last, everyone had left.

Maru waved to Jyoti as the car backed out of the driveway. She switched off the porch light, realizing with a pang the difference between light and darkness. The living room was empty. She took the receiver off the hook; whoever called could wait for Chander's return, she thought, realizing with a pang the difference between sound and silence.

She found Savitri on the bed, weeping, at last. Maru sat next to her, now holding her hand, now stroking her to calm.

Returning after rinsing out the dishes in the kitchen sink, Maru was relieved to see that Savitri had got up from the bed, and she could hear the shower running.

Chander was already back, and she could hear him talking to the people at Loewen-Gardner funeral home. They had not called back about his request for a larger hall for the service. Maru shook her head sadly, recalling one of e.e.cummings' lines: Dying is fine…Death is scientific and artificial and legal….

Within two years, Loewen-Gardner had cornered the community market with a simple strategy—they had bought two dozen copies of each of the holy texts, the *Bhagavad Gita, Koran*, and excerpts from *Granth Sahib* in Gurmukhi, and had placed the copies of the relevant text in very visible locations in the rooms whenever any of the communities held a memorial service. There had been a few gaffes at first, since they did not know which community used which text, but now they were super-sensitive and knowledgeable. There was no doubt they would figure out a way to find a chapel with five hundred seats. It would be foolish business sense not to accommodate the request of any customer who could bring, at a day's notice, five hundred mourners for a service.

Maru went to bid Chander good night.

When Maru returned to the bedroom, Savitri was on the ottoman, swiveling away from the dresser. Maru sat close to her, on the chair, from which she had removed Sharad's pajamas when Savitri was in the shower. They sat in silence, their knees touching, and their hands, the only light coming from the night lamp in the bathroom. From time to time, they heard the telephone being picked up even before the first ring was completed. Chander, bless him, was there, always there.

Savitri was calm now, and she spoke.

She related her stories with long pauses in between; once she walked to the window, drew open the curtain and stared a long time at the blue sky and wispy white clouds behind which stars occasionally appeared and vanished.

Once she paused so long that Maru knew she was weeping within. Maru wanted to hold her in her arms, and lull her to sleep, but not yet, not now. This was Savitri's time, not hers to control.

❦   ❦   ❦

The earliest memory I have is of the morning my father brought home the Daimler. We were all set to leave for school; Dinesh and Prakash were nagging me as usual, to hurry up. I quickly took the shoe brush and started brushing my black oxfords; hurry, hurry, they said, why do you bother to brush brush when it is going to get dusty by the time we turn the corner?

Just then there was the tooting of a horn; Appa, who never seemed to hear our screams and shouts at any time, heard the distant sound right away—he's like that, he has a car-ear, Amma often said; an ear only for his cars, she said when she was annoyed with him. Appa ran a used-car dealership. The trouble with Appa was that though he made good deals with regular vehicles, he could not bear to part with any of the beautiful cars he bought, and came a time when they stood in a row in what used to be stables, at the far end of the compound wall. One day, and this was before I was born, he decided that the only way he could have his beauties and yet not go bankrupt was to open a tourist service. Word soon got around among the foreigners that Appa's cars were the best. At any given time, there were twenty-five cars in our compound and a dozen drivers and cleaners. When the drivers took out the "beauties," they were dressed in livery, with shining brass buttons on red coats, and chauffeur's caps.

A green and gold car swung through the gates that had been opened by one of the cleaners. It glided along the circular driveway and stopped in the porch. "A Daimler," my brothers screamed, "a Daimler, dad, a real Daimler!!"

They danced around the car, touching the gold-colored chrome of the hubcaps, reaching for the gold crest on the hood. Appa joined them, "Isn't she a beauty?" he said. "Is it from the Maharajah's garage?" the boys whispered, climbing the footboard to peer in.

"Let's go, children, got your books, your lunch bag?" Appa opened the door for me, and bowed elaborately.

"Ladies first," he helped me in and got in beside me. "You boys can sit in front, with the driver," Appa said, "and we grand people will sit grandly at the back." He squeezed my hand. I swallowed my disappointment; I knew, and he knew that I knew, that he was saying all those grand things to console me for not being seated at the front. From the back, I couldn't see anything at all, for the windows were tinted on all sides, including on the glass between us and the front seat. I ran my hand over the luxurious leather upholstery, and he helped me reach the lace curtains that framed the glass in front of us. I stood up and stepped nearer the door. Houses and cows and rickshaws slipped behind us in the dark. I saw Kamini and her brothers walk next to the car and disappear behind us. I wanted to ask Appa if they could join us but our car had already glided past them. I waved out to them but of course they could not see me through the tinted glass.

"This is where the Maharani sat every time she went out," Appa said, "exactly where you are sitting, with her arm on the cushion just so," he set my arm on the silk cushion, and tucked another cushion behind me. "My little princess, who is one day going to be the sweetest, loveliest, smartest maharani in the whole wide world." He kissed me on the top of my head, and curved his arm around me, for the seat was way too deep and no number of cushions could help me sit straight.

🍁   🍁   🍁

After a pause, Savitri spoke again.

That was not my first memory, but I want it to be. One cannot change the course fate has mapped out, but one can control one's memory.

Or can one?

The first memory I have is of the day of my grandmother's funeral. I was three and a half, but I remember it as clearly as any memory can be.

She lay on a straw-pallet. She was draped in a beautiful silk sari. There were flowers in her hair and all along her body, not the little strand of jasmine she always wore, but thick garlands of tightly woven pink roses, silver strands of thread zigzagging across. The vermilion powder on her forehead was large and round. Her cheeks, as usual, were yellow with the turmeric paste she used instead of soap, but now, against her bloodless face, they shone with a golden glow. I waited for her diamond earrings to sparkle but she did not move and so I did, and the blue rays from them danced for me. She looked beautiful and peaceful as she slept. I was tempted to bounce on her as I always had when she pretended to sleep if I asked her for a story but I knew she was not asleep but dead. Amma had told me so, and I knew dead people never woke up. Amma told me that too.

I remember the scene as vividly as though it happened this morning. I was wearing a smocked dress of light blue mercerized cotton, with a cluster of red and yellow forget-me-nots embroidered on each side of the collar.

I now remember other details that have been embroidered around it since then, but that scene is original. I know, because years later, when I saw the dress in Amma's memento box—she kept a few of our baby and childhood things in a brown-painted steel trunk in the little room where she had her chest of drawers—I told her I remembered wearing that dress the day of grandmother's funeral, and she was amazed, and it has become part of the family's collective memory, recalled and retold along with all the details that I now know.

When Grandpa lay just as dead as Grandma now was, asleep and dead, Amma told me that dead people never woke up. And that was just a few days earlier. Amma had bundled me up into a car and we had taken a train to Bangalore. I hope Grandpa gets better soon, she said from time to time as the train trundled along, the train between Mysore and Bangalore was slow, very slow. And she sang some bhajans in her sweet voice, very softly though the others in the compartment said her voice was so lovely she should sing louder. It was dark by the time we reached grandfather's house in Malleswaram. The next day, night really, Grandpa died, and she made me stand at his feet and say a prayer, and said he would never wake up again. I don't remember any of this.

The funeral ceremonies progressed day after day, and on the seventh day, Amma's mother dropped dead. A fortunate death, everyone said, what *punya* the old lady must have amassed in her previous lives to have died so fortuitously, a *sumangali* who would forever be a sumangali. Because she died before her husband's soul had bade farewell on the tenth day, as souls did, she died a *sumangali*, a married woman; not a virgin or a widow but a married woman and no woman could have greater fortune.

Grandpa had died in the middle of the night. All of us, children, were woken up early in the morning and given the news. While we, the women and children, stood on the verandah, the men carried Grandpa away. Grandpa was a well-known doctor and so a great many friends had visited our house the day he was cremated.

When Grandma died, it was the newspaper report that attracted strangers to our house. For it was news indeed, that a woman should die within a week of her husband. People came from all over the city and beyond to touch her feet. More flowers had to be piled on her more strong incense sticks burnt around her pallet, and the cremation had to be postponed by a few hours to give more time for people to pay homage to this fortunate lady, who had died a *sumangali* despite her husband dying before her.

She had died around nine o'clock in the evening, but even so, the morning paper had the news on the front page, with grandfather's picture, because the family friend who had phoned in the news could not find any photograph of my grandmother. My grandfather's picture was not a recent one—it was a copy of the photograph that hung in his office room on one side of the front verandah. It was a massive hand-colored photograph in a massive gilt frame, and there he was, standing in the regalia of the Maharajah's court, with white trousers and black *achkan*, and a gold brocade shawl pleated and pressed down his coat front, a gold-edged turban, and the heavy gold chain that had been bestowed on him by the maharajah for his services to the poor and ailing.

The photograph, appearing on the front page for a second time within the week, brought visitors from far and away. Mostly women, married women, who came to pray that they too might have the good fortune of dying a sumangali at a ripe old age.

I remember that the pallet was placed on slabs of ice, and I remember the little streams of water that oozed from the sawdust across the black granite floor of the front verandah into the living room floor.

Many of those that came to mourn our loss and celebrate her life touched me on the head or cheek and told me how lucky I was to be named after this lucky woman. Savitri. Like the Savitri of old, Grandmother had persuaded the god of death to give her a boon; and the boon she had asked was to die a sumangali even though her husband had been cremated seven days earlier. And the god of death had to accede, for such is the power of a good woman.

Did the Savitri of old, I wonder, die a sumangali? That part of the story is never told, though we know how devotedly she served her husband's parents and how she won her husband back from the god of death and how she lived to bear many children.

Savitri sat quietly, her hands folded together on her knees.

Then it was Maru's time to cry. She cried hard and long. She went to the bathroom and sloshed cold water on her eyes. When she came out, Savitri took her by the hand and gently said, We have a long day ahead, let us rest awhile.

Just when Maru thought Savitri was at last asleep, Savitri spoke again, and Maru could hear the smile in her voice. Savitri said, "May be there is some method in divine madness, after all. I guess God's figured out that transplantation from one country to another strengthens women. Our men, they are so lovable, but they have no survival skills at all, don't you think? Sharad probably wouldn't have lasted very long if I had gone first."

Mooga

Mooga watched the hot water from the long thin instant-geyser trickle into the pail. He wondered if he preferred this geyser to the old system that he remembered very well, when the bathroom was a large room in a corner of the house, and the copper boiler was built against one of the outside walls. In those days, Gopal would stack the twigs that fell off the trees in the yard against the far end of the bathroom, along with fresh dry wood bought from time to time. Early morning, Gopal would take a few pieces of wood and twigs and light the fire from the other side of the wall. Everyone bathed in that room. When it was time for Mooga to bathe, Gopal would get hot water from the boiler with a brass *lota* and mix it with cold water, which stood in large pails near the boiler. After Vig had remodeled the house, everyone had their own bathroom, with a hot-water geyser that was fed by water from a tank on the terrace of the house.

It would take a long time for the pail to fill. But that was okay. He would wait. He should not twist open the tap any further. If he did, the water would flow faster but within seconds it would be tepid and then cold. Years ago Vignesh had told him there were little coils inside the geyser that heated the water real fast if it was allowed to trickle out, but those little coils couldn't keep up with their heating task if too much water came in. Mooga imagined they were like Slinky, moving shinily up and down as the water jiggled. At first Mooga could not understand the direct connection between the temperature of the water that came out of the geyser and the amount of water, but Vig had explained it with sketches on paper until he got the point. Slow, go slow and you'll get an endless supply of hot water; go fast and pouff, no more hot water.

Mooga now thought, May be if he had not gone so fast BEFORE, he would be different today. His mother had spoken often of how he had been BEFORE—crawling at five months, talking at eight months, repeating the alphabet all the way to V by the time he was fifteen months (he never could twist his tongue around W, she said that also very proudly), learning by rote Mother Goose from cover to cover, and even the multiplication tables long before he went to school.... If he hadn't gone so fast BEFORE, may be.... Or may be not. Amma often said the fever was a freak fever and nothing at all could be done about it at the time; by the time they knew it was THE fever, it was too late. But no matter, she always added, our Mooga is the dearest Mooga in the whole world and everything was hunky-dory and would always be.

Her sari-*pallu* was the softest of silks, and he often recalled how he would wrap it around his head. He did not remember much of BEFORE but he did remember the AFTER. She always had time for him, even though the younger children, Vignesh and Malini, needed her attention. She always had time to play hide and seek with him. He would run to her, stand to her left and bury his head in the long *pallu* of her sari, that smelt of potpourri and sometimes of cooking spices, and he would breathe deep deep and feel himself rocking in shallow warm water, safely cradled in soft soft silk. And she would turn round and round, peek under tables and chairs and behind cupboards looking for him. "Mooga kaanoomay, Mooga engay, kaanoomay." Oh how beautiful she was. Amma, my dearest Amma. Gone. No not really gone, for he could make himself real small and wrap his head in her silk sari any time he wanted. But the pail was almost full, and he had better shut off the tap and start his bath. He could smell Karuppan waiting for him just outside the bathroom. Karuppan never smoked anywhere near the house, but the smell of beedi clung to him. Mother's sari smelt of jasmine today. That was good. Jasmine was his favorite flower. He must remember not to use up too much cold water. The monsoons had not come this year. The summer had been a stinker, as Vignesh had said every time tanker-water had to be ordered, and now the winter was going to be one too. The water level in the well was always low and was mucky most of the time. They had long stopped pumping water from the well to the tank. If there was not enough municipality water from the taps, they bought water and the water-lorry came every week to fill the tank.

It was different when he was a child. All three children would stand in their underwear near the well on hot summer days. Gopal would draw clear water from the well, his biceps gleaming, and would pour it into a shining bright brass bucket, and Amma would whoosh slop the pail over them, and soap them, and rinse them off whoosh. And the children would slap their hands and chest and squeal with delight. Amma, beautiful Amma. Gone. Gopal too was gone.

❦   ❦   ❦

Neela watched the new man-servant, Karuppan, whom she had employed for Mooga after Gopal's death. She had misgivings about him. He did his work well enough, but she had heard him making fun of Mooga the previous day in the backyard, where the servants relaxed during their mid-morning break. Neela provided coffee and *idlis* for them every morning. Neela was familiar with the sight of the group sitting on their haunches in the courtyard, which stretched all the way to the vegetable patch bordered by coconut palms and banana trees. The two men, Karuppan and the gardener, had a smoke, and the two women chewed their *paan*. Then Ponni stuck a wad of tobacco into the side of her mouth. It was impossible to get her out of that habit. But may be Neela, selfishly, did not really mind because the tobacco, mixed with a dash of bhang, kept Ponni in a somnolent passive state. She did her allotted work very well, with slow movements of broom and then wet duster that covered every inch of the floor, unlike Chelli who tended to swish in a hurry leaving swaths of dust on the floor. Ponni seldom spoke, but Chelli spoke enough for all of them.

Karuppan was very efficient; Neela had made random checks on his duties, especially such things as taking care of Mooga's bath and massage. He placed the pails in the bathroom exactly right, the empty one under the geyser and the cold-water pail by its side so Mooga could mix the two without having to get up from his stool. Neela had checked on that the first few days. Yes, he did his work well, but he had no feelings for Mooga, the way Gopal had. How could he? Gopal had been with Mooga since his birth, and had taken even her under his wing when she came as a new bride to this house fourteen years ago. But Karuppan was here for the pay he got from her, which was a handsome package. He came punctually at eight in the morning and did not stay a moment beyond five o'clock.

May be she should give Karuppan more time to get used to Mooga, this thirty nine year old child who would stay with her long after her own went wherever their studies, marriage and careers led them.

When she was just married, she had been scared of Mooga's jerky movements and voice, and the lopsided appearance of his body because of his limp left arm and his large, right arm. Every morning he spent an hour on the lawn, flinging stones with his muscular right arm from the porch towards the gate. Gopal would then pick up all the stones into a wheel barrow and wheel it back to the side of the porch, making them into a neat pile for the next morning. His father, on his way to work, would stand for a few minutes as Mooga flung the stones, and he would say, Good work, son, soon you'll be flinging them over the gate and then we'll have to find some other exercise for you.

She found herself lost trying to place him. He was so smart in some things, like math and memorizing, but seemed dense in other things. Though he had a speech impediment, whenever he spoke slowly he was very articulate and logical. He had a fund of knowledge, often obscure details that he had amassed and retained. The fever had closed some doors, and there were other doors behind which he disappeared, often right in the middle of a sentence, and repeated the same words or phrase over and over again. Those close to him knew this usually happened when he was disturbed, and they steered him away to some mundane detail and that usually brought him back.

From time to time he made remarks so sensitive and insightful, they became family stories that others narrated on occasions.

Like the time her father-in-law was dying. He was a bossy man, and did not get along with his relatives and friends, always telling them what they were doing wrong, how they should do this, that or the other. He was a rich man, and generous, but his lashing tongue had resulted in isolating him from the rest of the family. However, during the two months he lay dying, the family came together; they and his friends visited often, and spent hours chatting pleasantly about childhood and politics and grandchildren; they brought little gifts for her and for Mooga, and talked to them instead of ignoring them as they usually had. And one day, Mooga had said, "Think how beautiful it would be if all of us could always live each day as though it was going to be the last day for someone in the family." Early in her marriage into the family, when she had not got used to their quarrels, Neela had treasured Mooga's little nuggets in her heart. Later, she knew the noisy quarrels had no malice, only a lot of hot wind. But when she was newly married, Mooga had been her mentor, telling her the family's stories and history, and all the little details about each member that helped her empathize with them.

Karuppan came in to massage his legs. Mooga missed Gopal, who would chatter all the time about what had gone on that morning. Karuppan was quiet and so Mooga had to do the talking. "Have you wiped dry the bathroom, Karuppa? I might have slopped some soap suds." Vignesh often asked that of

Gopal, adding how important it was that Mooga's bathroom floor be dry at all times. Gopal had to be asked often because Gopal still acted as though it was the old bathroom with rough-hewn stone slabs and not the smooth marble tiles of the renovated house.

"Yes, Moogaayya," Karuppan said, pouring some oil into the palm of his hand.

"My real name is Murugesh, but when Raja was a baby—you remember my cousin Raja, the guy who was here the other day wearing a bright green t-shirt?—when he was a baby, he called me Mooga, and the name stuck. That was BEFORE and so I don't remember, but everyone says so."

"Nice name, Moogayya."

"I would have preferred something else; mind you, Amma told me they thought of other Muruga names—like Kartik, or Subramanian, or Skandan—all of which I like better than mine, but they had already planned for three sons, and two daughters too, and wanted names that sounded just right together."

"Yes, Moogayya."

"The third son was to be named Mahesh, but he never was born."

"Too bad, Moogayya."

"But when you think about it, Mahesh doesn't really go well. Murugesh and Vignesh are brothers, but Mahesh is their father. Do you know stories of our gods? Karuppa?"

"Muruga stories we know, for he was of us, a hunter god, yes?"

"Of course, of course, you are perfectly right, very correct. But Muruga is also Kartikeya, general of Siva Maheshwara's celestial armies. But you are right, he is a hunter too, carrying his spear at all times. "Muruga Vel Vetri Vel," Mooga raised his hands and voice for the familiar chant. "I did not like my name at first, but I like it now. Do you like your name?"

"Who wants to be called Blackie?"

"No, no, Karuppa, it is YOUR name and you should be proud of it. You are special because there is no one else in the world like you. That is what Amma always told me."

"Yes, Moogayya, you are right."

"Right right right."

It felt good to have his legs massaged. Now he could lie back and become real small and wrap himself in Amma's jasmine sari and have a nap. For years he had held a real silk sari so he could fall asleep. He still had it under his pillow. But he seldom needed it now. He just had to close his eyes, not tight tight like he had long thought but lightly. Vignesh had taught him how to relax, how to lightly close his eyes so that the red inside was an even-shaded bright red and not a dark angry red, and to let his arms lie lax by his side, and lie on his back, and think himself into the silk. Amma, my lovely Amma.

But she was gone on a picnic, a long long picnic, and Appa had joined her too. It was a beautiful winter afternoon, and they were sitting under the Banyan Tree in the Theosophical Society Garden, the oldest Banyan tree in the city, perhaps in the world. Gopal was there too, gone, so many of them gone. But he had his Amma's silk sari, the color of slate gray clouds and a shining red border with woven gold lotuses, and she was always within hearing distance.

Mooga could hear Shailee's sarcastic laugh as she talked with Neela. Mooga usually liked joining Neela when he woke up from his afternoon nap. But if she had friends over, he did not get up. He listened instead; though he could not hear the words, he liked to hear the sounds of laughter, or lullaby some young mother sang to the child in her arms, or sometimes tears. Today it sounded like tears, not exactly tears but a whining. Shailee was a whiner. Mooga decided Neela would welcome an interruption, and got up. He used his walker, because it took him a while, after getting up from bed, to keep his balance. He joined them in the dining room. "Hello, Shailee, long time no see," he said his standard greeting, even though Shailee had been here just two days ago…

Shailee lived in the third block down the road, in a fair sized apartment. Her husband worked in a bank; she had an eight year old son; also a mother in law, who was the cause of her daily whining. "What's troubling you today?" he said, drawing up a chair and taking a biscuit from the plate, as Neela went to the stove to get him his coffee.

"What else? Always the same problem, Mooga, and always the same stalemate."

"If you can't beat them, join them," he said. "So he pays more attention to his mother than to you, you think. You should start paying attention to her, more than to him, and then what would happen?"

"Oh Mooga," she sounded exasperated, but could not help a smile. "That would be the day."

"People are like that, you know, everyone loves their mother more than anyone else even though they love others too. Mother is like an idea, a shrine. One needs that, Shailee, an idea, a shrine."

"Now, you are talking philosophy, Mooga; I think I like your humor better."

"And sometimes it isn't one's mother even."

Neela did not look back at Mooga but she smiled.

"What are you talking about?" Shailee was a little shrill. She thought they were saying something about her husband because she had a suspicious mind.

Neela was about to say whom Mooga meant when Mooga cut in. He saw no reason why Neela should say what she was about to say. He stuttered and said, "I was talking about my secret, Shailee, and I thought you knew about it. I carry my Amma's sari around."

Shailee looked at him, not knowing whether to laugh or not. "Like Linus," Mooga added. "Everyone needs a safety blanket to dream in."

Vignesh came home early. He brought a strand of flowers for Neela and a video for Mooga. He was all smiles and hunger. He insisted on Mooga joining him for another cup of coffee while he had his, and talked about the video he had brought. It was a war movie, all the movies Vig loved were war movies, and he wanted to watch it with Mooga that weekend after the children had gone to bed. He wanted Mooga to preview it during the afternoon next day. Mooga always watched videos earlier, and then again with Vignesh. That way Mooga could have his questions ready for Vig to explain.

Vig said this was a special kind of movie; real clips from old news coverage, real scenes taken by the soldiers and airmen and war reporters. "But the Germans always lose," Mooga said, "isn't there any in which they win the battle, even if they did not win the war?"

"The good guys have to win every time; and Hitler was a bad 'un, Mooga, a real bad un."

"That's what you always say, but even bad guys have to win some time. You can't toss heads every single time. And why can't we watch it this evening?"

"Because today there is a Special on last year's war. Interviews with those who were really there at Kargill; you remember how the government had enlisted the first widows of the war to campaign for them?"

Vignesh and Mooga sat on the sofa side by side and watched the regional news. The Veerappan story was dragging on. "But why did this actor guy go to the forest in the first place? Was it to bait Veerappan?" Mooga asked his daily question, which had no answer. His sympathies were with the bandit chief, who in his mind belonged to the dynasty of Sivaji Ganesan heroes who defied the establishment. That the establishment in Sivaji movies was the British and was today democratic India's made no difference. Every day he asked his questions. Why was this actor guy so important that everyone wanted the government to pay millions of rupees to ransom him? Were politicians making money out of this as they did with everything else? Was everything staged to get media publicity? Who was behind this media publicity?

Mooga asked his questions but was not bothered if there were no answers. Just as he had no answer to why he was on the side of smuggler-bandit Veerappan.

But he fell silent once the Special edition of the News started. There were clips from the battlefront, interviews with survivors, and families of survivors.

"May be it is okay for the boys out there—that is the way to go—tuptuptup gone in a moment instead of living on with some marbles missing."

Vignesh put his arms around Mooga's shoulder. "Buddy, I've told you this many times, you know. If marbles go missing, other marbles just chip in and get the work done; it is like a team having to play shorthanded when one of their players gets benched by the referee. The others simply take over and do his job as well as theirs. It works, always works, as long as one doesn't panic."

"But is the referee always fair when he benches players??

"Some judgment calls look real iffy, I grant, but there is always a reason; the more important point is that one never questions the referee. That is one of the basic rules of sportsmanship. You simply accept what the referee says and go right back into the game."

"Yes, yes, yes," Mooga nodded his head up and down. "Yes, yes, yes, way to go."

As the Special went on to feature the mother who had lost her husband and a son and still said she would sacrifice more sons if need be, Mooga stutteringly said, "I don't know if any mother can ever say that. That she would sacrifice all her sons too, if need be, for the country. Remember how much Amma worked and prayed all those years I went through one illness after another? You think any mother could just give up a son to guns and bombs? She'd rather die herself."

"Yes, Mooga, but it is far more difficult to live after losing a son than to die instead of him. Any mother would gladly die in place of her child. But that is not the way the game is played. To live after losing one's child, one's grown child, that is more difficult; you have to understand this woman's willingness to sacrifice."

Mooga did not say anything for a long time. Then he said, "Do you think he will bring *Sportstar* tomorrow?" Vignesh drew his brother closer and kneaded his shoulder gently. Mooga nodded his head all evening, side to side, repeating *Sportstar* statistics and test match prospects.

Three times a week, the Circulating Library man brought magazines of all sorts, some Tamil magazines, some English, mostly adult but he faithfully brought ChandaMama every week, which was fought over by the children. Vignesh diligently read *Newsweek, Time* and *India Today* and got upset if they were not delivered on time. The men-servants read the Tamil magazines and gave Mooga tidbits of fun and gossip. Mooga looked at all the magazines, poring over the pictures. He knew how to read, but preferred being read to.

Neela flipped through all the magazines that came, and mid-morning she read aloud whatever Mooga wanted her to. This was their hour—after the children and Vignesh had left for the day, and before Mooga went for his walk, bath and massage. Mooga had the memory of an elephant; whatever he heard and liked, he would repeat to Vignesh or the children later in the day.

Sportstar was Mooga's favorite; each day after Neela had read out to him, he looked at the pages they had read and repeated everything that Neela had read as though he was reading it on his own.

❧   ❧   ❧

Next day, Vignesh brought an even bigger gift for Neela, a flower arrangement with rose buds at the centre.

"Did you watch the video?" Vig asked Mooga, sipping his tea. "I forgot that we can't watch this weekend. The U.S. Open is on."

"Will Jimbo be playing?"

"No, Moogs, his days are over; it's Pete Sampras, out to break all records, and the Williams sisters."

"If there is no Jimbo, I am not watching. Jimmy Connors is the only one I like. Let's watch the video tonight, may be after the kids go to bed."

Vignesh patted him on the shoulder. "I have to go out," he said, "Neela, are you free today?"

"No," she said, "where is she singing and who else is going with you?"

Mooga smiled. He loved these conversations where each knew just what the other was saying. Vignesh answered that Mohan was picking up Pradeep first and then him, and that the concert was at Shastri Hall, which is why he thought Neela might like to join. She liked the acoustics in that auditorium.

Neela made room for the flowers on the coffee table by moving the newspaper, and declined. Both children had class exams coming up the next two days and she had to be home for them.

M'Lady of Lloyds, they called her, because she lived on Lloyds Road, and also because it sounded like Lords, and they thought themselves so. They were her knight-errants, her three musketeers. Her Lancelots, Mooga called them, reciting the Lady of Shallott: A red-cross knight forever kneeled/To a lady on his shield.

Others were not as kind. Neela's cousin Pratima thought it was downright disgusting, the way these three grown married men drooled like teenage groupies over the Woman. She refused even to name her. How can you put up with this awful obsession, she fumed at Neela. It is downright inexcusable, this abject adoration of the Woman. What delusions did they have she would like to know, these stupid, pea-brained men, who didn't know anything about music really until SHE turned up. And now they skipped work if necessary, and drove to wherever she sang, even if it was in some dingy mosquito ridden hall with cockroaches crawling up the chairs, like the hall in the boonies last weekend.

Still others laughed about it, ribbed them with dirty jokes. Ranga, the Woman's husband, often joined the jokers, for he was a sporting fellow, secure in his marriage. He was handsome, debonair, and usually very nattily dressed. But sometimes he liked to sport working clothes, especially when he drove to the music halls to pick her up after the concerts. While he supported her talent all the way and never grudged her the attention and fanfare she got wherever she sang, he himself was not fond of classical music. He would rather drive her to the auditorium and then come again to pick her up. He always came before the concert ended so that she would not have to wait, and he stood with the paid chauffeurs who waited for their rich employers, and was quite willing to cadge a cheap cigarette from them.

More than once he had been mistaken for a chauffeur, and asked by a socialite driving her own car to help her maneuver the vehicle out of the crowded parking lot. He had endless stories of such episodes, and especially of how women took him for a chauffeur and how elderly fans flirted with his wife as they escorted her to the car, not recognizing him as he slouched among other drivers.

Everyone liked Ranga, and he particularly liked the three musketeers, and used them without any qualms to do a great many chores for him. He was a middle-level business executive, and did not have the clout that the musketeers, with their hereditary wealth and social standing had to tear through red tape by speaking to the right person in the right way.

Mooga did not like m'lady. But he loved Vignesh, and Vignesh adored her. She was not particularly beautiful, but it was something about the way she carried herself; the way she sat ever so straight and still when she sang, unlike others who moved their torsos like rubber; the way she smiled at her accompanists when they played their solos; the way she smiled at some unseen person above her when she pulled off a difficult note, the way her fingers kept beat on her thigh, the way her zircon diamond necklace scintillated when she turned from left to right; the way she noticed special patrons as they came in, late as special patrons usually did; the way her artificial curls at the front of her neatly-coiffured hair curled further as she elegantly dabbed the sweat off her face during the second hour of the concert. Mooga saw all these through his brother's eyes, and he could understand Vig's attitude, even though he did not particularly like her.

The phone rang. Neela picked it up. It was Ranga, and he wanted to know if Vignesh could give his wife a ride to Shastri Hall since he had just been called away on work. "A ride to Shastri Hall? at what time?" Neela asked. Mooga said in an aside that he knew Vignesh had talked Mohan into driving because he never took his own car to that crowded place. Neela smiled to herself. How easy it would be to tell Ranga just that—'Sorry, Vignesh will never take his new car to that hellhole'—and let him find another chauffeur for his wife. But Neela said, Of course, he'd be glad to. He was home already and it would be no problem at all. And then she went to Vig, who jumped for joy. To him it was a victory that Ranga had chosen him over the other two guys, and he was already savoring the smell of the green-eyed monster that would soon be licking at the other two when he phoned them to say he would make his way on his own that evening.

Vignesh's illness came on suddenly. The cold he had been nursing for two weeks turned into pneumonia the night he came back from a business trip. He had inherited his weak lungs from his mother, who had inherited them from hers. Over the years, he had suffered bouts of bronchitis and mild pneumonia, but this bout left him weaker than he cared to show. He went back to work during the week and recouped strength all weekend, staying home and resting most of the day. Then it got worse. He spent three days at the hospital, recovered, and then was back in hospital within two months, machines drawing the fluid from his lungs. Neela and Mooga spent afternoons in the hospital with him; the children visited in the evening, first worried but later taking the hospital visits in stride, telling their father all about the day's events at school, even asking his help with their homework. Rajan, at twelve, was already in his school cricket team, and reveled in a ball by ball recap of the afternoon, and ten year old Rani was a chatterbox. Between them, they kept Vignesh's eyes bright with chuckles, and only Neela knew how tired he was by the end of the day.

Then, a few months later, Vig stayed in the hospital a longer time.

When he came home, he set up his office downstairs, in Gopal's old room, and he went to the main office only once a week. One or other of his partners came to him on the other days, for a discussion and update on the various projects.

The two computers that had been in study adjoining his bedroom upstairs were brought down. The changes made Mooga very nervous; he now stuttered any time he opened his mouth. He took to practising on his pellet gun. It was a pastime that Vig had initiated some years ago, to help Mooga improve his motor skills. In the wide circular lawn within the circular driveway in front of the house, he had set up the shooting range, a tall cement bench upon which stood a row of empty pop-bottles. Behind it was a movable screen of tarpaulin, to prevent the pellets from damaging the cars in the porch. There were two chairs and a patio table that could be moved to whatever distance they wanted. Mooga supported his disabled left arm on the table. It took him years to get a steady hold of the rifle, and he had never hit the target in all these years. Over the years Mooga had occasionally taken his cane and rifle, walked to the front lawn and sat there for an hour or two, while Gopal patiently picked up the pellets and watched Mooga painfully attempt to steady his arm. Now, with Vig in Gopal's old room, Mooga slipped out every day and wrestled with the rifle. Karuppan stood by, not always patient, and often itching to try it out himself. The rifle rather fascinated him. As a boy, he had lived near the Police Lines, and enviously watched their morning practice, and been enchanted by the concentric circles of red, blue and white painted on the green slope. He now figured that when he had settled into his job, he would ask Moogayya if he could try his hand at the rifle.

To distract Mooga from his growing frustrations, Vig tried to get him interested in the computer. Astutely, he asked Rajan to teach Mooga how to use the machine. Rajan wanted to show off his knowledge of spread sheets and computations. Mooga watched in awe, watched the boy's fingers move with lightning speed over the keyboard, watched the figures on the spread sheet refiguring themselves as they worked out fractions and percentages. But trying to do anything under Rajan's taking-it-for-granted instructions was frustrating; Mooga's fingers took their time moving, his disabled hand typed wrong keys and could not keep up with his able hand. He decided he could do complex computations faster with his pencil and head than with the computer. But the computer somehow brought back his ability to read faster than he had ever been able to read.

Cousins Jharna and Dharna came one afternoon, full of stories about the festive family weekend they had over Uncle Venu's seventieth birthday. But Jharna had suddenly fallen silent and Mooga noticed it. He went up to her and took her hands in his. "You are missing him, aren't you," he said. And she was. During the twenty-five years she had been married to Kesi, she had never spent a day away from him, except for the time their children were born. At family parties, he was always one of the loudest singers, and he had a belly laugh that filled the room. He had collapsed from a hefty heart attack last spring, his first, but heart problems ran in his family as respiratory ones in Mooga's. "Just think of it this way, Jharna," Mooga said, "Kesi is right here with us, and he is holding your hand, can't you feel it? Even when he leaves, he won't go far. He'll just go back to his picnic bench under the Banyan Tree. Don't worry, just wish yourself there and you can feel his hand—remember the big scar he had on the back of his right hand?"

Mooga had said that and he meant it too, but that day when Vignesh lay down as soon as he came back from work, Mooga suddenly had doubts about the picnic tables under the Banyan Tree. What if they weren't there any more? What if the Banyan Tree was not there? It was years since he had seen it.

He remembered one time there had been a tertiary trunk that had a huge hole in its middle. Next time the trunk had vanished; just regular pruning so the main trunk can be healthy, his father had said. Ten or twelve years ago, a huge storm had ripped part of the tree and that made newspaper headlines. What if the Banyan Tree was not eternal, what would happen to the picnic if the tree fell down? Also, he would never tire of the picnic but others were not like him. They got bored easily, they always wanted something new, something different. His father had been like that. He had no hesitation selling one car and buying another. So may be his parents weren't there any more. Amma always tried to please Father, and she would have packed up if he wanted to go someplace else.

Mooga took out his mother's sari and sat on his bed for a long time.

That night he held the sari for a long long time. Over and over again he said the same thing—Amma, don't go away without telling me where. And take care of Vig. Take care of Vig.

Next day he came to Neela as soon as the children had left, and sat at the dining table. She had a towel in her hand, for she usually went for her shower as soon as she had seen them off. But one look at Mooga told her he was upset. She waited for him to open up.

He came straight to the point, as was his custom.

"I am worried, Neela, very worried about something. You know about the picnic, right?"

"Yes, of course, Mooga, under the Banyan Tree. Jharna told me about it; she said she was so comforted by your words. You do know to say just the right thing, Moogs."

Mooga rocked himself waist up.

Neela waited, but he said nothing.

"May be you can talk to your brother this evening about whatever is on your mind," she said gently.

"I can't, he cries so easily."

It was true. Vignesh cried easily and unashamedly. He cried when watching movies; he cried when the children threw themselves at him when he returned from his business trips; he even cried whenever Neela got dressed up in one of her lovely saris, with jewelry to match and asked him to help her with the hook on the necklace. When Neela was all dressed up, anyone would feel like crying, Mooga thought, she was so beautiful, but Vignesh went right ahead and cried. He did not cry noisily the way children did, but very silently. Tears would just stream out of his eyes, and he would wipe them away on his shirtsleeve or shirt tail, just like a child. He never cried for more than a minute but yes, he cried easily. He cried during the Olympics coverage along with gold medalists as their flag went up to their national anthem. Even the way the evening sun shone on the top of trees, even a line from a poem was enough to get him going.

"That is why it is so difficult to hold anything against him, isn't it?" she said, and Mooga knew what she was thinking.

"It catches us right here," Mooga held his hand to his heart, "I don't think he knows that, else he wouldn't," and Neela knew why Mooga never cried.

"It is all right to cry, Mooga. All of us have that child inside that needs to cry and laugh." She said it more for herself, knowing Mooga was more child than man much of the time.

"What if they've gone away someplace else? What if the Banyan Tree has rotted and fallen? How do we know it is still there?" Mooga's voice had an urgency she had not heard in a long time.

He was so perturbed, Neela hastened to soothe him. "We'll drive down this weekend, Moogs, yes, it is years since we went there. Let us do it, let's have a picnic there; the children will love that, and it will be good for Vignesh too."

"No no no," Mooga almost screamed, and Neela caught her breath, knowing what he was thinking.

The coconut-tree climber had come. The children and Mooga watched him as he slipped the rope loop around his feet and deftly hoisted himself up. In the straw-woven basket that was slung around his waist, he dropped a few green coconuts; the brown ripe ones he threw down from on high shouting at them to keep away, even though they were well away from the tree, their eyes turned upward till their necks ached. Thud, thud, thud, they fell, thud thud thud. But Vignesh was not on the verandah to watch the lithe dark climber or hear the thud thud thud. He was in bed, even though it was a beautiful Sunday morning.

But when Mohan came by and in the course of conversation said m'lady was singing at the Music Academy, Vig's eyes lighted up. He would go, of course he would go. But he did not tell Mohan that. He waited till Mohan left and then he whispered to Mooga about his plan. If they started early enough, they could get a parking spot close to the auditorium.

You can take my walker, Mooga said, and I'll take my walking stick. We can make it, he said, caught up in the excitement. They hushed up on hearing Neela's voice. She came in, placed the car keys on the dresser and clapped her hands. "I am taking you guys out today," she said. "A surprise."

The brothers looked at each other. Which of them was going to talk her out of whatever she had in mind? Which of them should break the news about their own plans? "Look at this," she drew tickets out of her handbag. "Music Academy seven o'clock." Tears welled up in Vignesh's eyes.

They were late for the concert because the doctor came just as they were about to leave, apologizing for the delay, and listing mishaps that had kept him on the run all morning. He stayed on for the coffee and biscuits Neela offered (hoping he would decline) and chatted. He seemed satisfied with his patient's condition; he prescribed an energy tonic, and left at a quarter to seven. By the time Neela dropped them off at the door of the auditorium, found a parking spot and came into the lobby, they were forty minutes late. Vignesh went in wheeling his walker, and took an aisle seat; two friendly persons by his side moved up to make room for Neela and Mooga. M'lady had her eyes closed as she reached for a high note and did not appear to have seen them. But after the pallavi, she nodded to her accompanists, who paused to see where she was going. She started on a kirtanam in Hamsadhvani, which took everyone by surprise since it just was not done at that point in a concert. It was a familiar song addressed to Vigneswara, which she had meant to sing at the beginning of the concert but had not because she had noticed that Vignesh was not in the auditorium. Remover of obstacles, Vigneswara, giver of wisdom, dancer divine, victory to you, she sang.

It was late December. Vignesh came home after staying at the hospital for a week. The basic daily routine of school and meals continued, but in the last month, much had gone a-kilter. Tutors were engaged to help the children with their studies because Neela was at the hospital all day. Instead of going to the vegetable market twice a week, Neela now had vendors come by with vegetables, and instead of her leisurely shopping at Nilgiris, she phoned in all her grocery orders and had them delivered from the new store that had opened in Alwarpet. A small new refrigerator appeared, for Vig's medicines, and then a sterilizer for his needles and I.V.; a nurse came late evenings and stayed till morning. The large family room that had been the site of so many family parties over the years was transformed into Vig's room. Neela moved a bed in and slept in one corner while the nurse had a couch in the other.

The family room was one of Vig's proud achievements in the house that he had re-built. The rebuilding had been done so fast after his father's death, it was as though Vignesh had been planning it ever since the first day he had joined the School of Architecture. As years went by, and he had got married and Rajan had come along, his plans had been refined. The new Raj Vilas, named after his father, Rajaraman, rose on the foundations of the old. It was an imaginative design. For sentimental reasons Vignesh wanted the old house, which had been built in the 1930s by his grandfather, to be still visibly there despite the renovation. So the ground plan of the old house, with its stodgy plain rectangles was retained. But around it, Vignesh had designed curvatures that gave it a graceful sweep. Balconies and windows curved around the exterior so that windows could be opened or shut at different times of the day to let in optimum sunlight and receive the sea breeze. Inside walls curved and spiraled. The house had a shell-motif for some, with its cased walls and curved staircase; others thought they could see the symbols of western music and harps and violins in the striations on the curved walls.

On the terrace stood a weather vane and a structure that looked like a cross between a circular chimney and an observatory dome. Vig considered it his pièce de résistance. The walls of the dome had four large horizontal vents, to receive the breeze, and there were vents in every room that could be opened or shut. A series of levers controlled the vents at the top, closing or opening them as needed, to draw in the breeze from the right direction, depending on the seasons or times of day. It was an ingenious concept, not quite practical, but Vig tinkered with it periodically, sure it could be the answer to harnessing the sea breeze.

For Mooga, he built a suite on the main floor. Mooga's bathroom was an experiment done for the heck of it, as Vignesh said. It was almond shaped, with the toilet in the narrow curve at one end. The sight was always good for a laugh to those who saw it the first time. But it had been carefully designed so Mooga could hoist himself holding the railings on each side. Such details could be seen in every room: the built-in stone grinders in the kitchen on counters that were lower than the standard height, so women could lift the heavy cooker off the gas stove with ease; the single rough hewn slab in Neela's marble-tiled bathroom so she could rub her heels clean against it, especially in the winter when the soles of feet get chapped and collect dirt.

The family room was an architectural show piece, as everyone who ever stepped into the house agreed. It was strange now to see the sofas pushed away, and Vig's bed set up, with tables and shelves and rocker forming a semi circular wall around the bed.

During the day, Vignesh seemed fine; he took care of himself, shaved, bathed, read the newspaper, walked in the garden with Karuppan and Mooga. And he saw videos, his favorite videos of war and adventure stories. Karuppan now did double duty, as personal valet for both brothers. He seemed to like that variation, and he loved watching videos with Vig.

In the afternoon, Neela took to driving the children back from school. She had figured out that the half hour drive would make the children feel close to her again and make up for the evening hours that had been taken away from them as they wrestled with their homework and tutors.

Every afternoon, when it was time to leave for the school, Neela came in, did one or other little thing—rearranged the pillows, neatened out the bed-sheet, cleared the side table—and then said she was off to school; "and don't you sneak off anywhere when I turn my back," she'd say, running her hand through Vig's hair or taking his hand to her cheek.

She was always cheerful when she came back with the children. She often took them on a detour, picking up some needed grocery, or giving them a little outing, to the park or bookstore. The children always had a story to tell Vig about the drive back from school.

They often stopped at Fast-Track, a video and bookstore, to check if the long awaited Harry Potter volumes had come. It was a small store, opened by Sandhya, an ambitious woman who thought there was scope in a children's bookstore, and if there wasn't, well, she'd just have to educate people into real-izing there should be. She stocked the classics, fairy tale collections from every culture, and in several languages. The business side of it was a losing proposi-tion but she was a wealthy woman, with a wealthy husband. However, the ide-alistic side was prospering; the story telling program was going well; she engaged grandmothers to come in and tell their stories in Tamil; she engaged professionals to read the classics; she engaged performers to act out fairy tales and Tenali Raman stories in nearby cheris. She did everything with great enthusiasm and little organization, but through word-of-mouth the audience grew. The performances took place on the verandah of the store, and were public enough that passersby stopped, and regulars helped out with donations.

Neela and Sandhya were good friends, and Neela welcomed the chat while the children looked around, playing with the video toys that Neela on principle refused to buy. Her children had grown up with more books than toys. At the end of the half hour or hour, Neela dropped a twenty or fifty rupee note into the donations box, out of which storytellers and performers were paid. The donation box was Neela's idea. Another of the lessons that had to be spread, she maintained, was that toys did not have to be bought and thrown away, but rented for a short time so that their appeal held. Between the two of them, they hoped that they could reinvent the waste of birthday parties among the well-to-do where spoilt children were taken to private clubs or restaurants, and expensive gifts exchanged, gifts that were soon thrown into closets already burgeoning with toys. But, since business was business, Sandhya did stock all the inane hundred rupee toys that the children gave and received at these wasteful bashes. Neela urged her that if she did not get around to running a toy-exchange (Sandhya said her clientele would never agree to their children using hand-me-downs) she should at least have a donation-box for toys so that the rich could contribute to poor children's pleasure. Neela had many ideas, and Sandhya's response was always the same—Become my business partner and we will make the world a better place. Otherwise, don't nag me with your ideas.

❦   ❦   ❦

"I can't take it any more," Mooga said one day to Neela in the kitchen. "Those war movies are so awful, why does he watch them? I just can't take it."

"You have to, Mooga," Neela said, "till Vignesh gets better, you are the man of the house and you have to take that and a lot more."

She said it quietly, and Mooga wanted to cry because she looked so tired, so alone.

And so he couldn't talk to her any more.

But he was deeply disturbed.

Every day he sat on the oval lawn, rifle in hand, but making no attempt to shoot.

What if, what if there was no Banyan Tree after all? He had stood watching quietly watching his world dissolve at his father's funeral. "No electric crematorium for me," Father had said several times over those last two months. "I don't want to be stashed away on a biscuit plate in a baker's oven. Give me the logs, sandalwood, mantras said under the sky, the whole works." And they had. There were six priests, all the men in the family had rushed in by train and plane, and they had cremated him with due honors. Mooga blanked out as he thought of the scene. No, he remembered. Father had been carried three times around the pyre, counterclockwise ("in life, all circumambulations should be made clockwise, and in death the other way," the chief priest had intoned) and placed on the pyre, Vig had circled the pyre, holding the clay kumbha pot on his left shoulder three times anticlockwise and his uncle had struck the pot with a sharp knife each circle (symbolizing life's waters oozing out, the priest intoned) and Vig had held the flaming torch behind his back, and lighted the pyre (Oh Agni, receive my father's body). And he walked away, as prescribed, without looking back. Mooga had seen the flames soaring skyward, carrying Father's spirit to heaven while Father's body turned to ashes. He had known then that Father's spirit could now go wherever it wanted to and that he would join Amma's under the Banyan Tree, and that the picnic would continue forever.

But now, he started having doubts. It was a documentary on Viet Nam, which also featured the Arlington Cemetery and the War memorial plaque that shook his belief. May be he was wrong. May be the others were right, those others who buried their soldiers day after day in coffins so thick and buried so deep deep in the earth no spirit could ever fly away to the sky. They made sure body and soul would stay together in the coffin they buried deep deep in the ground, so they could rise when angels blew their trumpets. Then each bodyandsoul along with a million other bodyandsoul would march up Beach Road all the way to the High Court and wait till the blackrobed judge came in and started the grand trial. That way, bodyandsoul would be together at all times and also all of them would be together at the High Court and all of them could go together to the Banyan Tree so no one would ever lose anyone else.

But they had cremated Father and Amma, and now they had no body, and may be Father and Amma had left the Banyan Tree because Father was like that, he got bored easily, he lost his patience easily, he got angry easily, and Amma dear Amma was always trying to please him and would do whatever he wanted done.

And what was worse, he couldn't make himself small any more and wrap his head in Amma's soft silk sari. He was a grown man and the man of the house until Vignesh got better. He could not cry, he could not forget himself in *Sportstar*. Karuppan did most of the reading aloud nowadays but Karuppan knew to read only Tamil, and so *DinaMani* was the only newspaper he could read from.

Sometimes Mooga's head ached as though it would split. Always at night. During the day everything was okay; and though he got goose pimples every time Neela said to Vignesh, Don't sneak away anywhere when I turn my back, there was nothing he could do.

But Neela wanted him to be the man of the house. That tired, lonely look in her eyes, that she hid from Vig and the children, impelled him. He put away his rifle. He put away his silk sari-blanket. He had to take on the job he was assigned. He became the man of the house and organized each day as the man of the house should. All the servants had to report to him every morning, and tell him what their special jobs for the day were. The gardener, who came three times a week, had to tell him just which section of the compound he would sweep and which beds he would weed; the driver, who came twice a week in the afternoon, had to report to him; Karuppan had to call him out whenever any vendor came so Mooga could check on what was bought and how much paid to whom. Even the children had to show their satchels before going to the school van, so he could see they had sharpened their pencils and taken the right notebooks. Everyone went along with him, treating it as an escape from the somber air that swirled around the house.

Mooga also took charge of his demons. He got the driver to drive him to the video store and bought a copy of two of his favorite Sivaji Ganesan movies—*Kappalottiya Tamizhan* and *Veera Pandiya Katta Bomman*. The store owner asked him many times over if he was sure he wanted to buy them and not just rent them. That weekend, after lunch, he introduced the children to his hero. He told them about these heroes who defied the British, KattaBomman who refused to pay agricultural tax to the British arguing that native land cannot be taxed by a foreigner, and V.O.Chidambaram, another revolutionary who built ships and defied the British. The children listened politely, and Rajan, who loved word play said he was rather at sea with all that history. Wisely, Mooga cued the video to the scene of Veera Pandiya Katta Bomman's fieriest oratory, and with his spirited preamble, got Rajan mildly interested, though Rani was not too taken up by Sivaji's girth and loudness. Mooga figured they were too young to appreciate the finer things of life, and stopped imposing film-declamations on them. Later, he told with Vig with some dismay that children nowadays did not seem to know what Britain had done to India.

Vignesh watched the oldie movies with him in the afternoon, to humor Mooga. In a way, it did Vignesh some good. It brought back memories and they relived them and laughed over their childhood escapades. Neela was usually a silent listener.

One day, the talk turned to Father, and Vignesh said, "I have been wondering about Father's last days; you remember that day he talked about Mooga and made me promise something?"

Mooga and Neela remembered it well. Father had said he was leaving enough money for three generations to enjoy every comfort without lifting a finger, but that money alone was not enough to keep a family together. One needed a sense of commitment, and he wanted Vignesh to promise he would take care of Mooga for the rest of Mooga's life. And Vignesh had held his father's hand and Mooga's and had made the promise.

"At the time, it seemed so right. May be because of it was so much like death scenes in movies that we loved to see again and again. But later, it made me sad, to think that Father didn't have any faith in me at all; I mean, didn't he know I'd take care of Mooga with my life if need be? What was the need for a promise?"

Neela gently said, "Don't look at it that way. Don't we take so many vows when we get married? Do you think they too are needless?"

"But now," Vig continued, "I see it differently. He had a point."

"Don't worry, Vigs," Mooga said. "Don't worry. We know. You know Neela and you know me. We don't need to take any vows. We are a family and will stay so. But don't you run down Father or my Sivaji for taking vows and making others do so."

Mooga had spoken in a clear, slow tone, but it had cost him a huge effort. He started declaiming Sivaji Ganesan's *Parasakthi*, and then like a phonograph record with a scratch, kept on repeating the same line.

Mooga could not sustain that first burst of energy of being the man of the house. He started losing his temper with servants. And when that happened, he stuttered terribly, which made him even more frustrated. He either kept to his room till lunch-time or hobbled round and round the huge circular driveway all morning, mercilessly torturing his malformed legs, refusing his walker and walking stick and Karuppan's help. Karuppan worked in the garden at this time, keeping an eye on his charge without intruding. Only Sivaji movies seemed to calm him down. Soon, his book shelf carried every available video in which his hero had acted. He bought himself a video player for his room and orated with Sivaji all the way through, often mouthing the words even before Sivaji did.

One day Vignesh taught him how to surf the net. Let us do some traveling, Vignesh said, and opened Alta Vista.

It became a bonding hour for the men in the family, as they called it. Rajan, Vig and Mooga spent the hour before Rajan's bedtime going places, the capitals of the world, two capitals every day, with one of them repeated the next day. That way, when they saw anything a second time, Rajan and Mooga competed as to how much data they could regurgitate from the previous evening. Rani occasionally joined them, but got bored and went off to bed. Mooga liked the game, liked repeating from memory the tourist places and descriptions even before the words appeared on the screen; loved watching pictures of Jama Masjid and Red Fort slowly unrolling on the screen; Rome's Coliseum and the fountain which made Mooga sing "Three coins in the fountain" in his slightly cracked voice; Cairo's Alabaster Mosque, London's Big Ben and Buckingham Palace with its statue-like guards. These four cities were his favorites, and he went to them even in the afternoons, till Rajan found out and complained how unfair that was.

It was then that Mooga found newly-started Google. He would tell Neela or anyone who cared to listen about his findings, about the various attempts on Mount Everest, about the ozone layer and global warming, about insects and butterflies. Then, he suddenly stopped talking about his trips on the computer.

He had asked Google about lungs, and had followed every link there was. He read about non-small cell lung cancer and small cell lung cancer, and wondered which one Vignesh had. Vig had been a chain smoker since his early twenties, and he had not given up even after his first diagnosis. Small-cell lung cancer, Mooga had thought, hoping it meant the danger was small. Then, when he knew it did not mean that at all, he prayed that it be a carcinoid tumor, which could be removed and thrown away. But he knew it could not be because the doctors would have known what to do, after all. He withdrew from the computer and into himself.

Mooga took out his mother's sari. He asked Neela for safety pins. "I need a shawl," he said, "and may be this will become a fashion of the day, if I wear this gorgeous silk shawl to the Music Academy." Neela said she could sew it on the machine in a jiffy, and she did, with fancy stitches for edging. "It is a rather long shawl," she said, "but may be you can use it as a blanket."

Mooga took to wearing it as a shawl during the day and a blanket at night. He saw his Sivaji movies and seemed to have lost interest in the computer for a while. But then he became an addict, sitting at the computer, with his shawl around his shoulder. He spoke less and less, and when he did, he used a loud cheerful voice, which Neela knew was to hide his inner demons.

Realizing that the computer had something to do with Mooga's withdrawal, Neela tried to surprise him at the computer. The first few times, she did not succeed, for Mooga closed Netscape before she could look over his shoulder. But one day, she chanced upon sheets with his scrawly writing as he sat in front of a blank computer screen. Knowing she knew what he had been reading, he said very loudly, "I was thinking that if I were a little smarter, I could make a million bucks correcting web pages for these people. Like the home pages of some of these leading research centers refer surfers to see the following site's, site apostrophe s, when they mean "sites." Is that dumb or what, one would think heavyweights like them would know when to use apostrophes and when not to. I have found "it's" instead of "its" in at least ten web pages, can you believe it?"

He would have gone on, but Neela zeroed in on his notes. "Sloan Kettering?" she said.

He then showed her the countless links. But she turned away. "What is the use of all this, Mooga, we already have the best doctors in the city."

"Look at this," he said, pulling another sheet of his notes. "Shark cartilage for Stage IV lung cancer, this guy says it helped him. Don't you think we should try?"

He was the man of the house. And he could see that the house needed some serious help. But he did not know where to go from there. Vig's business partners were fine people, but he could not interrupt their visits with Vig. Neela's friends, who dropped by early afternoons, were extremely nice people, but Neela was always around when they visited. Mooga missed Gopal. With Gopal, he could give expression to his thoughts and fears, and even though Gopal never had answers to any problems, the very act of expressing them aloud often helped Mooga figure out answers. His practice shooting got worse, as did his stuttering.

When Neela's parents made their customary once-a-fortnight phone call, he suddenly knew what he had to do. Neela was always upbeat with them; not letting on about the toll Vig's illness was taking on her own health. She did not tell them too much about Vig either, always saying it would take some time but he was improving by the day.

"Why do you say that?" Mooga asked her, "why don't you tell them the truth?"

"Why worry them? What can they do anyway?"

Neela's parents lived in Tiruchi, their home town to which they had retired the previous year after thirty five years in the Civil Service; working for the Central Government had meant a move from place to place every few years. But they had never been posted in Chennai. They came once a year for a visit, and they phoned once a month. Now, since Vig's illness, they phoned twice a month, but they clearly did not know the more serious details.

One afternoon, when Neela was away, he figured the man of the house had responsibilities. He phoned Neela's parents. Her mother answered. Mooga had carefully rehearsed what he was going to say. He first asked about their wellbeing. Neela's mother said they were thinking of going to Delhi for vacation. All the niceties that Mooga had rehearsed fell out the window. Sternly he said, "This is no time for a vacation, Aunty. We need you here." Because he was surprised at himself for having taken such an audacious step, he stuttered, and she could not make out his words. She got scared and called out to her husband. This time, Mooga spoke very slowly—"Uncle, we need you. Vig is not getting better, not getting better at all. Neela needs you, but she does not want to bother you. So don't talk to her. Just come. Give her a surprise." And he hung up. They rang back right away, wanting explanations. Mooga stuttered his way through his thoughts. "Don't ask her, just tell her you are coming."

They rang up that evening and said to Neela that they were planning to drop by on their way to Delhi. Mooga was jubilant that he had got through to them. I am the man of the house, he told himself, I am getting to be good at this.

❉   ❉   ❉

When Neela's parents saw how things were, they were dismayed, but quickly took charge of themselves and the house. Forget Delhi, they said, this was going to be a long-overdue vacation with their grandchildren.

Their arrival swiftly changed everything. There was laughter and quarrels in the children's rooms. The children went back to their old ways of bringing home their friends, playing cricket on the front lawn, watching video cartoons with playmates.

The servants again started shirking their work, knowing Neela would now be on their tail, and not silent and unheeding as she had been till then. It was good to hear Neela's angry reprimands, it felt good to have the mistress and children running around singing and scolding again, and if only the master would be his old self, everything would feel right as rain.

Neela's mother arranged for their cook to join them. Rukkamma had been with them since just before Neela was born. Having lost her husband when she was barely seventeen, Rukkamma had come from her village to help out with the new baby but had stayed on and become part of the family. She had faithfully followed them all over the country and Neela had developed a love for cooking on the side, as it were, for what attracted her to the kitchen had been Rukkamma's story-telling. Neela's parents, being part of the elite social circuit of government bureaucrats, would often be away late evenings, and Rukkamma became a surrogate mother for the children.

Rukkamma now took over the kitchen without missing a beat. She made a distinct place for herself—she ordered the servants around, establishing her precedence over them. She endeared herself to the children by making hybrid foods—stuffing mashed carrots and peas in toasted sandwiches, pouring melted cheese over spinach—so that they did not clamor for fast foods and take-out pizzas any more. She formed an instant rapport with Mooga.

The kitchen had two doors—one to the dining room and one to the back verandah. Vig had thoughtfully built a long narrow wooden table with a granite top, with benches on either side, so the servants could have their coffee-break snacks there when it was raining. But the servants did not take to it—they preferred sitting at a distance from the house, so their conversation could not be overheard. Their favorite place was near the well, where there was a tap and the clothes washing area with a raised cement washing-stone. Similarly, Vig had built a large cement sink in the verandah so one could wash utensils standing. But Ponni did not care for it. While she grudgingly washed the porcelain cups and saucers there so they could be safely put away, she preferred to do what had been done for years—to stack all the vessels to be washed in a large cane basket and to carry it to the well-area. There she sat on her haunches and scrubbed the pots and pans with coconut coir and ashes, or tamarind, or shikkai powder, as needed, let them dry in the basket, and had Chelli carry the basket to the verandah and put them away on their proper shelves.

The table on the verandah became Mooga's favorite spot after Rukkamma's arrival. He sat with her as she chopped the vegetables, and ate chunks of carrots and tomatoes, and chatted with her. He had a lot of questions, about her various travels to places where Neela's father had been posted over the years. She was all too willing to talk about Chandigarh and Delhi and Jaipur and other places. She loved a half-cup of coffee every forty-five minutes, and she would bring Mooga also a half-cup and take a break from work. Within days she had figured out the main points about Mooga. "We are of a kind, Mooga," she said, "you and I—our lives are all wrapped up in the people around us; we live for them and because of them. That is the way it is, and thank god for that."

One morning, Rukkamma came out of the kitchen, ladle in hand. "Now, why hasn't that wretched girl come yet? I don't have a single saucepan that I can use. Ponni, bring the basket here, and be quick about it. I don't have all day."

Just then, Chelli arrived. "I know, I know," she lifted her hands in self-defense. "I know I am late, but if you had seen what I saw you would have just curled up and not come out for a week. Ammamma, what a tragedy!" Having set the stage for her drama, she waited until Ponni and Karuppan came to the verandah. Then she related what had happened that morning. Chelli lived in a three-storey row-apartment block, low income housing that the government had built all over the city, including on the beach.

The woman in the flat upstairs had killed herself, drinking a bottle of acid. Her insides had all burst on to the stairwell, there was blood and vomit all over the stairs, her three children were crying their hearts out without anybody to take care of them, the police had cordoned off the whole block. Chelli went on and on with her graphic descriptions till Ponni told her to shut up.

But why? Karuppan asked repeatedly. What led to such a terrible act? Neela asked.

How could she do this to her children? Rukkamma shouted angrily. Did her husband beat her? Ponni wanted to know. No, not at all, Chelli said. He is a nice looking man. Ponni snapped, Nice looking men also beat their wives. Don't ever fall for a good-looking man, you little fool.

Chelli ignored Ponni. She said the husband seemed a good man, never beat or shouted at his wife, brought expensive gifts for her and their children whenever he came home. He worked abroad, may be Singapore, may be Andaman or Maldives, but he was away a lot, and his wife thought he had a woman out there; that was what it was all about, she did not want him to go abroad, and when he refused to stay home, she drank acid.

Neela said, You say he provided well for them, and took care of their welfare. She should have been satisfied with that and not suspected or accused him. Really what does it matter as long as he loved them and took good care of them?

Ponni said, About men's roving eyes, what would Neelamma know? She has a husband who worships the ground she walks on, bless his dear heart.

Mooga kept silent through all this, his head nodding up and down.

Later, that afternoon, as Rukkamma was shelling peas for the afternoon snack, he sat next to her and asked, "What do you feel, Rukkamma, when you listen to such stories as Chelli's? Do they live on another planet? What she said seems so unreal."

"We have led such sheltered lives, I can see what you mean about how different they are, the working classes and their drinking and beating and carryings on. But it happens with us too, Mooga, it happens everywhere. You and I have been lucky, is all."

"Do you really think yourself lucky?"

"Oh yes, oh yes. One has to be really lucky to belong to this family."

"Tell me about your mother, Rukkamma, do you remember her?"

"To be honest, I don't. I don't remember much of anything that happened before I came to this family. May be because I don't want to remember."

"Don't want to remember what?"

"I really don't remember. And I don't want to. It is not a happy thing to be poor, Mooga, never to have enough to eat, always giving your share to a younger sibling and feeling guilty if you didn't. It is all a blur, and I really don't want it any other way. My life is here, in this family."

Mooga was intensely curious about Rukkamma. She had always turned away from questions about her life. But today she opened up. Mooga said, "I can't remember much of BEFORE because I am not all here, but you are so together, so yourself." She said, "You are all here, Mooga, and don't let anyone tell you otherwise. You are a caring intelligent man, and we are lucky to have you here." She went on. As for remembering, she was the same way. She just could not remember much of her BEFORE; she was the eldest; her father was always tired or angry, her mother was always tired and pregnant. Her husband? She could not remember him at all, it was a blur, getting married, getting widowed. He was much older, had some ailment, seizures, she never knew him, never knew him as a husband, though she had lived for a whole year under the same roof. He was both weak and violent, and he would take to his bed with a cold for days on end. It was all a blur, except for her mother-in-law saying she wanted her son married so there would be someone to take care of him after her days, but Rukku, born under an unlucky star, had killed him, and now Rukku could go back to where she came from. And so she had returned to her father's house, one more mouth to feed. Now you know why there is no point trying to remember.

Mooga nodded his head up and down, up and down. He was clearly overcome and needed time to sort out things out. Later that day, he came to her in the kitchen and said in his raspy voice, "I am glad you didn't drink acid, Rukkamma. I am so glad you are here."

Rukku had her private interests—periodically she would disappear at ten in the morning. This trip was a bonanza she had never thought she would get—the big city of many temples. Twice a week she completed her snack and lunch preparation by ten o'clock. She took a second bath, put on a clean sari, tied her still-wet hair in a tight knot, and spent ten minutes with Karuppan, asking him about the route. She took copious notes on a sheet of paper that she tucked into her sari at the waist, and away she went, coming back after the others had their lunch. She came back full of excited stories of how she had first lost and then found her way to the temple. Did you know? she would say to Mooga, who was always a willing listener, that goddess Karpagamba in the Kapali temple came as a peahen (mayil) and Siva assumed the form of a peacock and they danced here and that is why it is called Mylapore? On her return from the Parthasarathy Temple, she told Mooga excitedly that she could actually see on Lord Krishna's image the scars from Bheeshma's arrow. Mooga was more interested in knowing in what century the temple had been built, how tall the gopuram was, and whether the scaffolding was still all over the exterior of the temple. But Rukkamma had not noticed.

After a couple of weeks, she decided to explore the more distant temples, and also that she wanted to feel fresh and clean so she could feel devout. So, instead of taking the bus, she took an auto-rickshaw to the temple after checking the route with Karuppan so that the rickshaw driver did not take her a circuitous way. She would return by bus.

"Oh, I want to go again," she said to Mooga one day even as she came in, "I want to take you to Vadapalani. It is a Muruga temple, Mooga, a Muruga temple. And the god is just so wonderful, you should see the way he stands! He is so beautiful! You must come with me."

"I'll take a rain check on that, for the day you come with me to a cricket test match."

"Will a cricket match give you *moksha*? If you would just spend some time reading about our gods, Mooga! Instead of preaching to me that St. Thomas the apostle opened shop in Cochin within years of Jesus dying."

"In 52 A.D. to be precise. He converted the Jews who were already there. Which means Jews came to India long before the times of Jesus."

"Oh, you are impossible. Why don't you read about how Sankara traveled from Kanya Kumari to Kashmir or how the Cholas sailed all the way to Thailand and Cambodia?" Rukkamma tucked her pallav end tighter into her waist and walked away.

Neela's father had a scholarly bent and though he was a silent man and kept to himself, he took charge of the children's homework and studies. Neela's mother was a lively, efficient woman for whom even water boiled faster than it did for anyone else, as Neela always said in her teen years when she was run ragged at the pace at which Mother did anything she started.

With an orderly routine re-established, Vig seemed to improve. He started working at his desk again, and even had the driver take him to his office once a week.

"There is one great project I need to complete," he said one day. "A theater in our own front yard." He was intent on building a small open-air theater where Sandhya could develop her story-telling initiative. He showed Neela and Mooga his drawings. Mooga took one look and said, "Were you thinking of a miniature Greek theater with circular slopes and all?"

"Am flattered you should think so, Moogs. The ancients in every culture had the principles of acoustics well in hand; nowadays people think they don't have to bother with those principles because of microphones and stuff. In my world, there will be no microphones. I might even install some gadget that will electrocute anyone who dares fix a sound system in this theater. Yes, this is totally miniature—just five tiers each eight inches high. Max capacity eighty kids, not the thousands of olden days"

"Fifteen thousand was the usual seating capacity of a Greek theater," Mooga said. "The Attic theater could seat 50,000 people, imagine!"

Neela took one look and said, "Looks impressive, but our neighbors will not be pleased to have an open-air theater next door. Sandhya's busiest times are weekend afternoons, and all her storytellers come with music."

"The neighbors would prefer story-telling to an apartment block, don't you think?" Where there had once been large houses with a compound wall, apartment blocks were mushrooming. Narrow lanes that had once led to four or five exclusive houses on either side now had ten apartment blocks of four or five storeys, each with ten or twelve apartments. The traffic on these narrow lanes was horrendous, and once in a while, someone opened a bank or mini-mall in one of the blocks, worsening the flow of traffic.

"I don't know," Neela said dubiously.

A few days later, Vig called the whole family to his office room. He set up his projector screen and took out a sheaf of transparencies. "Observe everything carefully and then tell me what else you'd put in." The stage was a circular marble slab, with two shallow steps leading down to the ground.

"If you made it black," Rani said, "we could draw hopscotch lines with white chalk."

"Good point, Rani, I will think about it."

"If you put up a basketball post on one side of the stage, we could practise there," Rajan said.

"Hmm, Let me think about that."

On one side was a dressing room, and on the other a storage room.

"Why not a bathroom?" Rani wanted to know.

"The shows will be just an hour long. Do you think it is necessary?"

Neela said, "Neighbors won't like *cheri* children tramping in and out at all times of the day."

"They will have to change their attitudes, don't you think? Vig said. "As will the cheri children too—they will have to learn they can't spit and pee wherever whenever."

"So we do need a bathroom," Rani said triumphantly.

"Changing the world is a lot of hard work."

"Rajan and Rani will grow up and be gone in no time, and then what will you do? You will all have the time in the world to change the world for the better."

"I will be too busy taking care of my no-good husband and brother-in-law to take on any extra work," Neela laughed, but she knew what he meant.

Vig placed the next transparency. "Voila," he said, "if you don't want a theater, you can have this terraced garden, green slope at the back, which will be there anyway, and potted plants galore, in which you can grow any flowers you please." Colorful flowers appeared on the next transparency.

"Eek, who can water so many flower pots?" Rani said, always practical.

"Faded flowers so close together will stink up the place," Rajan said.

"It is just so beautiful," Neela said.

The way she said it made Vig's eyes brim over.

Vignesh stopped getting better. It took a lot of effort on Neela's part to get him out of the house, to take a walk around the garden, to go for a drive along the beach.

"It is time we thought of something to celebrate," Neela's father said one day, "may be it would cheer up Vignesh and Mooga to have a family celebration, like Rajan's thread ceremony."

"Oh, yuk," Rajan said, "who wants to have a thread on one's body all the time?"

Rani rounded her eyes and said, "Rajan is just a kid. Janu's brother is sixteen, and he still doesn't have it."

"Yes, yes, let's have it," Mooga said excitely. And let us invite everyone; may be even Uncle Pooran will come!!!"

Uncle Pooran was an uncle by marriage, a retired army colonel with a fierce army moustache and many fierce army stories about Kashmir, Bangladesh, Pakistan. As boys, Vignesh especially had loved his stories, and had admired the ease with which he would spit out a string of expletives in his native Hindi. Uncle Pooran was still good for a weekend of lively tales of action and battles, and Mooga was sure he would do Vignesh a world of good. Now that the Veerappan incident was over, Mooga found he did not have much to talk about in the afternoons when only he and Vignesh were around.

The date for the ceremony was fixed, invitations sent, cooks and caterers arranged. Grandma and Rukkamma marveled every day at how easy it was to arrange for an event in Madras. Everything was only a phone call away. A couple of phone calls brought the sellers to their doors. Not like the olden days, when one's sandal soles were rubbed off with walking down lanes in search of suitable shops and the best quality of dals and vegetables.

And yes, most invitees said they were coming. Uncle Pooran was on his way, threatening to stay a month, he said. Cousins in the city offered to host out of town relatives; they dropped by more often than usual for a chat about what else they could do to help. It was indeed going to be a gala time.

One day, Rani wanted Grandpa to tell them the story behind the *upanayanam* ceremony, but he said there was nothing to tell; except that she would never know what Vignesh would whisper into Rajan's years because that was between Brahmin men alone. Which sent her into a tantrum. Out of which Grandfather pulled her, whispering into her ears the first line of the Gayatri after making her promise she would tell no one but no one, cross my heart and hope to die. What else, what else, she wanted to know. It was just a ceremony of initiation into adult Brahminhood, so one could take part in religious rites, Grandpa said. That was it, really o truly o only that and nothing more.

But Mooga understood. Where is *Sportstar*? he said, where is today's *Sportstar*? I have to read the cricket results. Have to. Have to.

Next morning he was back on his walks, hobbling painfully, feverishly round and round the circular driveway around the lawn. And Neela knew that he knew what she had known the moment her father had said "It is time we thought of something to celebrate," and which she had submerged to the very bottom of her being. She knew that he knew she had known all along. She knew what memories had risen to the surface to torment him with the future he did not want to face.

Vignesh had told her the night of his father's death, after everyone had come back from the cremation grounds, had bathed and had a bite to eat and had sat in silence listening to soft taped *veena* music interspersed with soft *bhajans* and then had retired with heavy hearts each to their own room. He had told her of how Mooga had thrown a tantrum at the cremation grounds about wanting to light the torch to the pyre. "I am the eldest son," he had screamed. "I get to do it." Uncle Girish had firmly led him away, saying Mooga was not qualified, he did not know anything about rituals, did not even wear his sacred thread, how could he call himself a Brahmin?" Mooga, he of elephant memory who could dredge up facts and figures out of deep depths in his brain, had in his blinding deafening grief trusted his uncle, forgetting that he too had been invested with the thread the same day Vignesh was, even though he had never worn it since or done the prescribed Sandhya Vandanam.

Vig did not tell Neela of how he had stopped Uncle Girish from manhandling Mooga, how he had grasped Mooga's arm, had forced him to look at his own eyes that were red with unshed tears, how he had said, Moogs, look at me, look at me, Moogs, we are in this together, it is my hand but your heart, your courage that's going to tell my hand to do what has to be done. Get it? And he did not tell how Mooga had calmed down right away and had stood, quietly watching the ceremony.

Vig did not tell her either how that moment had changed his own life, how it made him take charge, had forced him into his father's shoes. His career had hardly taken off the ground, and even though he now had a wife and baby he was still rather carefree and irresponsible, but that moment when he took on Uncle Girish, he had stepped into his father's shoes, and he and everyone around him knew it beyond doubt.

Mooga now started spending hours over *Sportstar* issues. The issue featuring the U.S. Open, bought by Rajan at the time because he loved the pictures was Mooga's favorite, more so because no Circulating Library man would want to take it away. He looked keenly at the pictures and read to himself the captions under each. He read the way he had read BEFORE. Sitting near Amma as she cut vegetables or churned cream into butter; he would trace each word with his forefinger and spell them out letter by letter; Amma would say the whole word if he could not, and he would repeat the sentence up to that word. Now he had to fill in for what Amma would have said. "Cee-eee-ell-eee-bee-aar-a-tee-eee-ess celebrates, Pete Sampras celebrates h-i-s his v-i-c-t-o-r-y victory, Pete Sampras celebrates his victory o-v-e-r over…"

One day Rukkamma said she was going to take the whole day off on Wednesday, which was Full Moon day, and some women she had met at Kapali temple (to which she went often because it was within walking distance) had told her about a bus trip to the Shakti temples. There were three temples to Shakti, and if one went to all three on the same day, one would get any boon one asked. "What boon do you want so badly, Rukkamma?" Mooga teased her. She tsk-tsked. "Don't make fun of me. God knows one could do with some prayers around here." She would leave Tuesday morning and go to the house of one of the women in the group; that woman's son would take them to the bus depot at three in the morning, and the bus would leave for Meloor.

Neela quietly had the driver take her to a sari store and bought three saris. One was yellow, for the first temple, to be offered to Ichcha Sakthi with mangoes; the second was red, to be offered to Gnana Sakthi with jackfruit, and the third was green, to be offered to Kriyaa Sakthi with bananas. She gave them to Rukkamma with the required fruits on a plate. "May Ichcha Sakthi grant you your heart's desire, Rukkamma," she said and left the back verandah.

Rukkamma turned to Mooga and said, "I need no boon for myself. I have everything I need. It is for my child. True I did not carry her in my belly, but she has been in my arms since the day she was born." She paused. "I have a favorite story, Mooga. It is called 'And He made the milk to flow.' You remember how *gopis* would nurse each other's babies?"

"They did?"

"But of course, haven't you read the Putana story, how baby Krishna sucked the life out of her when she came to nurse him with her poisoned breasts at Kamsa's behest?"

"Is that how it happened? because it was a custom for them to nurse each other's children? Now the story makes sense, perfect sense."

"Well, there was a woman who came one day and wanted to nurse baby Krishna.

Mother Yasoda knew the woman was childless, but gentle as she was, she handed the baby to her. The barren woman held the baby to her breast, which instantly spurted so much milk that baby Krishna drank and drank so much he did not want any milk the rest of the day."

Mooga leaned forward. "I don't remember reading or hearing this story. Where can I get a-hold of it, Rukkamma?"

"You can't, because it is mine, just mine. I used to hold baby Neela to myself and dream about the story. It comforted her to suck when she woke up in the middle of the night, as it did me. My poor baby, look how she is suffering. What can I do for her now, except pray to the goddess, Mooga. Ichcha Sakthi grants all one asks for."

Mooga stuttered. "You are so lucky, so lucky. I wish I could have your faith."

Rukkamma was about to go back into the kitchen, but then she sat down at the table.

"Once there was a man who lived in the southernmost district of India."

"Kanyakumari?"

"Okay, he lived in Kanyakumari. His children were all grown up and his wife was dead. One day, he called the whole family and said, 'It is said in our Scriptures that everyone should bathe at least once in the Ganga before his death. A dip in the sacred river cleanses us of our sins and we will go straight to heaven. So, I have decided to go to the Ganga.'

They said, 'It is a long way, Father. Stay with us so we can look after you in your old age. When the time comes, we will pour Ganga water on your lips, and sprinkle Ganga water on you to speed your way to heaven.'

But the old man had made up his mind that a full dip in the sacred river would earn him moksha. So he took a sturdy staff, telling his grandchildren it was so he could beat snakes and scorpions out of his way, even though everyone knew he was already so old that he needed the help of a staff.

He walked northward. He walked and walked. Every night, he slept where he could, ruined temples, under the trees, in abandoned huts. By and by he came to a river. Joyously, he ran to it, crying, 'Oh sacred Ganga, I am so happy to have reached you. Cleanse me of impurities so I may go to heaven when my hour comes.' He stepped into the river, and came out feeling cleansed and pure. A man was passing by and the old man said, 'Brother, I feel so happy to have washed away my sins in the Ganga.' The man laughed and said, 'Brother, this is not the Ganga but river Kaveri. Ganga is farther north.'

So the old man walked north. He walked and walked.

At last he came to a river. Joyously, he ran to it, crying, 'Oh sacred Ganga, I am so happy to have reached you. Cleanse me of impurities so I may go to heaven when my hour comes.' He stepped into the river, and came out feeling cleansed and pure. A man was passing by and the old man said, 'Younger Brother, I feel so happy to have washed away my sins in the Ganga.' The man laughed and said, 'Elder Brother, this is not the Ganga but river Krishna. Ganga is farther north.'

So he walked and walked northwards.

At last he came to a river. Joyously, he ran to it, crying, 'Oh sacred Ganga, I am so happy to have reached you. Cleanse me of impurities so I may go to heaven when my hour comes.' He stepped into the river, and came out feeling cleansed and pure. A man was passing by and the old man said, 'Little Brother, I feel so happy to have washed away my sins in the Ganga.' The man laughed and said, 'Elder Brother, this is not the Ganga but river Godavari. Ganga is farther north.'

And so it went on. Tapti, Narmada, Soan, Yamuna.

Now he was very feeble. Even his staff, instead of helping him, felt too heavy in his hand. He fell ill. And walked fewer and fewer miles each day, asking every passer-by for directions, for he could no more figure out which was east, west or north; daylight became a blur, night utter darkness for the stars were too far away for him to see. One day, the man he asked said, 'Grandfather, you are very near the river Ganga. It is just there, may be another five hundred steps and you will be there.'

'Thank you, child,' said the old man. 'I am here at last, to dip my body in the holy river and cleanse it of all sins.' The man went his way. A few steps further, the old man fell down, and could not get up. He dragged himself—there was the river. He could see the sun shining on it and the ripples dancing all white and gleaming. 'I will rest a while,' he said and drooped his head, never to rise again.

And Hari received his spirit and said, This man I shall take directly to Vaikuntam, for he has bathed in the Ganga not once but seven times."

Mooga spent most of the day on the lawn, even though the day was hot and humid. He was intent on hitting the target. Karuppan dared not speak to him, but Mooga suddenly said, "Hit the goddamn bottle, will you?" And he handed the rifle to Karuppan. Karuppan excitedly took the rifle. He hit the target after twenty or so tries. "Beginner's luck, Moogayya," he said, apologetically, jubilant within. "You try, now, Moogayya, try now. I have put Muruga's power into it. Murgua Vel, Vetri Vel." Mooga tried. Karuppan held Mooga's left arm firmly on the table, and helped aim. The shot was much closer to the mark. "We'll get it, Moogayya," he said excitedly. "You are almost there." They tried again and again, nearer but not quite. It was time for afternoon tea. "We will get it," Karuppan said. "We will. Or my name isn't Karuppan."

❦   ❦   ❦

Neela phoned Malini about the upanayanam. Malini said right away that she would come down for at least a week. Mooga guffawed when Neela told Vig that Malini was coming.

"Oh, no," he said, "she will do her usual round of tailors and craft shops and miss the ceremony altogether." "Don't be mean," Neela said, with a laugh, because Mooga had summed up Malini in those few words. Malini was married into the Silicon Valley. She had gone there soon after her wedding, which was before Vig's. For the first eight years, she had not come home at all, busy having one child after another, and completing her Chartered Accountancy program. When her youngest was a year and a half, she had brought all three in tow, and then said, Never again. And Mooga said, Amen, because the six weeks had been one long visit to doctors' offices, each child falling ill in tandem; the older two being quite the brats, wanting their macaroni and cheese and French fries between bouts of diarrhea; and the youngest losing weight so rapidly, Malini spent more time trying to change her return ticket than with family members, who came daily from various parts of the city to visit with her.

After that, she and her husband traveled at different times, one staying at home in the Valley with the children while the other spent two weeks visiting. Then, the last few years, she had come for three weeks every second year. It was always the same. She would arrive in time for the Music season, have a taxi at her service all day, and be chauffeured from one sari store to another, from one craft complex to another, from the blouse-tailor to jacket-tailor to the place they stitched falls for the sari; then in the evening, she would go to one or other dance concert.

In between, she would make rushed visits to family and friends, and to her in-laws, all the time bemoaning how little time she had, how hot the weather was, how she had to work so hard back in California, weighed down, what with the house (3,600 square feet) and work (both she and her husband earned six figure salaries) and children (they were long past the age of heeding their parents). She would bring her old saris and blouses and give them away to the servants, who loved her visits and waited on her hand and foot, and then she would go back with two huge suitcases of new saris and blouses and beautiful handicrafts.

Mooga was not surprised when she phoned a few days later to say that she could not make it—the boys would be right in the middle of exams, and at her work-place it was tax-time.

Rajan's upanayanam ceremony brought the whole family together. For four days, the house was festive, special cooks hovered all day over temporarily constructed stoves and giant pots and pans, and there was an endless stream of visitors to visit the guests who had come from out of town. Vignesh was his old self, full of energy and laughter, but Neela alone knew and Mooga alone sensed that he was washed out by early evening and ran on will power. Two days after the ceremony, after all house guests had left, he took to bed, his adrenaline rush over.

Mooga took charge again, concentrating exclusively on his brother, now that Neela's parents were there to do everything else. He learnt just what medications had to be administered when. He was always at the nurse's elbow as it were from the time she came in the evening to the time she left in the morning. He slept in Gopal's room, on a cot that was brought in every night by Karuppan, who made it into a bed with mattress and pillow.

One day, Karuppan came in with joined palms as Vig and Mooga watched the News. "Moogayya," he said, and stopped. Wasn't Vig his master? "Ayya," he said to Vig.

"Yes, Karuppa." Vig guessed a favor was going to be asked. Karuppa was not normally given to obsequiousness. "Do you need some leave? Someone getting married in the family? May be you yourself?"

"Ayya, you have been very kind, very generous. But…"

"Go on, don't be afraid, what do you want? An advance?"

"Ayya, I have joined the army, I have to report next Monday."

Neela was on the phone in the dining room; Vig was sleeping; he slept a lot nowadays. Even though she spoke softly, Mooga could hear her because he knew her voice better than his own. "Yes, I am so glad everything went off so well, and so glad you could come," she was saying. Then in response to what the other person said, she said, "Yes, I was hoping we could come to one of your concerts, once he gets better…" her voice trailed off and then picked up again, "It was so thoughtful of you to send a card last week. I wish he could have spoken to you at the Upanayanam; he would have loved that; you know he always looks forward to meeting you. Do come by some time."

Mooga could have cried listening to the plea in her voice. Cards were not enough, didn't that stupid woman know that? What is the use of having a heavenly voice if one couldn't know that cards were not enough?

Mooga sat at the table, waiting for Rukkamma to bring him his afternoon coffee along with hers. The house was quiet. Neela had gone to bring the children home, and had said she might be late because she had to drop by Sandhya's bookstore. Vig was asleep. Rukkamma came with two tumblers of steaming coffee and some *murukku* pieces for snacking.

They talked about Vig's plans for building Sandhya's theater in front of the house.

"What is the first story you plan to tell when the theater opens, Rukkamma?" Mooga said teasingly.

Rukkamma said, "Once there was an old woman who lived in a small town. She lived alone; her husband and children had died long ago; she made her living grinding flour. She lived frugally and saved her money, for her greatest desire was to make an offering of twenty one silver pieces to her *ichadevata*, Badrinarayan. Any time she thought she had enough money, she went to the silversmith and asked him if she had enough to buy a silver coin. Sometimes he sent her back, saying it was not enough. Whenever he said she had enough for a silver coin, she got it from him and wrapped and tucked it in her sari at the waist, came back to her hut and safely buried it in a corner near the little pedestal where she had placed a little replica of her lord. Years went by; she now had twenty coins. She was now nearly blind, and people did not come to her with their grain. You are too old, they said, you don't see that you are mixing dirt with the flour. So it took her a lot longer to earn enough for that final silver coin. One day, she had it, twenty-one silver coins. She was ready to go on her pilgrimage. She took her walking cane, slung her spare sari into a cloth bag, and started on her journey. A group of pilgrims took pity on the old blind woman and allowed her to walk with them. Day after day they walked; at night the others had money to buy their food; sometimes they remembered to share it with her, and sometimes they forgot. At long last they reached the foothills of the Lord's mountain. The old woman climbed up the steep slopes, her feet stumbling on stones, which she could not see. The others helped her when they remembered, but they sometimes forgot. At last they reached the top of the sacred mountain. So eager were the others to pay homage to the Lord they had come so far to worship, they left the old woman and said, 'We will go ahead. It is not far, just keep going.' The old woman stumbled step after step towards the sound of the temple bell. Perhaps I am going deaf too, she thought, when the sound became more distant. She heard someone walk by. 'Son,' she said, 'tell me the way to my dear Lord. I have a come a long way to worship my Badrinarayan.'

'Here,' he said in a gruff voice, 'let me lead you.'

'Your voice scares me,' she said, 'but you must be a good man, to help an old woman.'

'I am an ugly man, eaten away by leprosy,' he said, 'and if you had eyes, you too would indeed keep away from me.'

'I now know why your voice is so rough, son,' she said, 'forgive me for being so unkind. Have you seen my Lord?'

'Yes,' he said, 'I live here. I was born here. The only thing I can thank your lord for is that some pilgrims throw a coin or two in my direction once in a while.'

'You are blessed, son,' she said. 'Our scriptures say, There are numberless sacred spots in the heavens, earth and the underworld, but there is none equal to Badrinath, now or ever.'

They came near the temple. 'I must leave you, now,' he said.

The old woman walked up, and a priest rang the little bell he had in his hand and said, 'Now now old woman, blind are you? be sure you don't touch me, I am a priest.'

'Pundaji,' she said, folding her hands in salutation, 'I have come a long way to see my lovely much loved Lord, and to give him my offering of twenty-one pieces of silver.'

'Ah,' said the punda in a sweet voice, 'you are indeed lucky that I was passing by. Come.' He led her up the steps on the side of the temple, and sprinkled water on her and chanted slokas in Sanskrit. 'Now, make your offering, here is the sanctum, here is a plate with flowers and fruits.'

The blind old woman carefully undid the knot in her sari and took out the silver coins. She dropped them into the priest's palm, and said, 'Tell me, in which direction is He? to my left or to my right?'

The priest neatly tied the silver coins into his dhoti at the waist, and said, 'To your right, old woman, to your right.' And, chanting slokas, he walked away, towards the sanctum, which was behind them.

The old woman turned to her right and raised her arms in worship to the Lord, ecstatic that she had fulfilled her heart's desire."

"The scoundrel, the knave, he deserves to be hanged," Mooga said, angrily.

Rukkamma said, "Mooga, the words of the story are the same for everyone, but we read it differently, you and I."

"Guess what I found out today on Mr. Googles," Mooga said to Vignesh one afternoon when Vignesh awoke from his nap. "Our banyan tree really is the oldest in the country. It is 450 years old, which makes it fifty years older than the one in Ramohalli, which is 28 kilometers west of Bangalore. But is it bigger?

I have to figure that one out. One site says our tree's roots cover 40,000 square feet, and another site says the circumference of the roots is 251.65 meters, and the tree is 12.2 meters tall and covers an area of 4670 square meters. 4670 square yards itself would be, like, 43,500 square feet; so one of the sites is wrong, I guess. But listen to this," he looked at the sheet in his hand, and said, "The Bangalore tree covers three acres. One acre is 4840 square yards is like…about 40,000 square feet. Which means it is three times larger, oh come on, do you believe that?"

Vignesh smiled and shook his head. "You sure are having a lot of fun with the computer."

"Yeah, it's great," Mooga thought of all the details he now had about Vignesh's illness, but brushed them away. "May be I haven't got the hang of it, but all I get from other search engines is a list of hotels around the world with Banyan or Tree in their name, but Google, wow. Like, you remember how that huge trunk or branch or whatever it is called had been lopped off one time when we were kids? Well, in 1988, says Google, there was a big storm which blew down a centuries old Banyan tree in the Theosophical Garden, but they managed to save it. It couldn't have been our tree, could it? When did we last see the tree?"

"No, absolutely not, our tree is eternal." Vignesh said it in a tone of certitude, with more emphasis than was needed. "Our tree will always be there."

Hesitation trembled in the air for a nanosecond, and then both brothers met it head on.

At the same time they spoke:

"Vig, I've been meaning to ask you…"

"Moogs, our meeting place, remember?"

"That's what has been bothering me, Vig."

Vig knew that already, relayed to him months ago by Neela, and now it was time to find out more about it.

"You know Father, how impatient he gets, always on the move, and how Amma always wants to please him…"

"So?"

"What if they have gone away some place else? What if they have found some other place, like the Niagara where you can watch the waterfalls forever and never get bored, or Nanga Parbat, from where you can see the whole world stretched out below you. I mean, I'd like to see those places, wouldn't you?"

"Sure would, so?"

"Vig, you are being purposely dense. You know just what I mean."

Vig was stalling for time. "So? Sure we'll be able to go everywhere. The Alps, the Andes, the rain forests of south America, the Kalahari desert, just think what a blast it is going to be!!! I can't wait to join them."

"But what if they are not there? How are we going to find them?"

"I will find them, Moogs, and I promise we'll keep some places for going only when you come too."

"But how? If they have already left the banyan tree?"

Vig chose his words carefully, knowing Mooga would never forget whatever he said now. "I think once we leave, we get more powers than we now have. I am sure they will know a little before I do when my time is to be. And I think wherever they are they will just fly back to our place before I can say 'ready or not here I come.' I am absolutely sure of that."

"And you still believe the referee isn't unfair to bench you?"

Vignesh sighed. "I hope I can stay around a little longer. Man, it will be damn hard on the kids otherwise. School life is so tough nowadays; remember how we played hookey and got away with it, how I could get into any College I wanted without carrying a donkey's load of pressures the way it is for kids nowadays?"

"They are bright as a button," Mooga clicked his fingers.

"Yes, and everything has turned out okay, don't you think, Moogs? Neela's parents being here has taken a load off our backs, don't you think? The kids are okay, you are okay, and Neela…"

They were silent a while.

"Do you think I should get them to promise they'll stay?" Vignesh asked hesitantly. "With you and Neela, we know that is not necessary, but tell me what you think about speaking to them."

Mooga looked back at him seriously. "I'd like to think about it, Vigs. I think you should speak to them, you know how people feel about living in their daughter's house…. God knows why the custom ever evolved the way it did, and God knows it is high time we threw away some of these stupid beliefs. But I'll have to think what and how and when. Mind you, I think they will stay because it is not as though they don't have their own money and servants and house to go back to any time they wished. When you have your own household, you can stay in others' without feeling uptight."

"And another thing, Moogs. Rajan is young, so young. True he has his sacred thread and all, but he is a child, a mere child. I'd rather you did all that, you know, all the rigmarole of rites…."

Moogs looked away. If only he could go to his *Sportstar*, this thud thud at the back of his head and the pit of his stomach would go away. The floodtide of tears rising up would recede. His able hand clenched the other in a vise. *Sportstar* was no good any more. Players were crooks, the same as politicians. Their lockers were stashed with laundered money. They sold their souls to the fixers just like any politician anywhere. Even the White House rolled out the red carpet to the Lincoln bedroom if one gave them enough money. He had to be on his own now.

"When the time comes, Vigs, their Grandpa is the only one who knows how to take charge of all that, and I guess we should leave it to him, just as we are leaving the children and Neela to his care. And when you think about it, Vigs, it is not only the eldest son's duty but an honor, don't you think, to do what has to be done?" An honor that had been taken away from him. And which Vigs was now trying to set right. Vig knew that Mooga knew that. Eldest son, he had said.

"It would be good if you could do it…he is just a child…"

"Just promise you won't fly off to see the Rain Forest without me."

"Deal." They shook hands on it, with a laugh and a smile as they had with other deals over the years.

When Neela returned from school with the children, the brothers were in a lighthearted mood, and the house seemed brighter. "Have you been hatching some plot behind my back?" she asked teasingly. "Yes, of course," Vig said, the words flowing easily and lightly. "We were making plans about my trip to the Banyan Tree. I'll run it by you later tonight. Let us go have a cuppa tea with the kids' having their cocoa.

978-0-595-39438-8
0-595-39438-8

Printed in the United States
49962LVS00003BA/277-285